"What Is Tiny Legs Wiggled Against His Palm.

"A hermit crab. I thought you might want a soul mate."

With a shake of his wrist, he tossed the shell into the sand. "I prefer my crab to be of the Alaskan King variety, served on a plate with drawn butter."

"I guess you don't want the little guy?"

He glanced at the small crustacean hiding deep in his borrowed house. "He doesn't appear to want me, either."

"There's no accounting for taste."

"His or mine?"

"Both."

Clayton sighed. Dandelion flowers and hermit crab pets. Buried beneath her tough exterior was the real Mikki—a wide-eyed optimist who found beauty in the things most people ignored. At this moment she seemed far more dangerous than a gold-digging schemer out to steal the Hawthorne fortune. If he wasn't careful, she just might steal his heart.

Dear Reader,

Welcome to a new year with Silhouette Desire! We begin the year in celebration—it's the 10th Anniversary of MAN OF THE MONTH! And kicking off the festivities is the incomparable Diana Palmer, with January's irresistible hero, Simon Hart, in *Beloved*.

Also launching this month is Desire's series FORTUNE'S CHILDREN: THE BRIDES. So many of you wrote to us that you loved Silhouette's series FORTUNE'S CHILDREN—now here's a whole new branch of the family! Award-winning author Jennifer Greene inaugurates this series with *The Honor Bound Groom*.

Popular Anne Marie Winston begins BUTLER COUNTY BRIDES, a new miniseries about three small-town friends who find true love, with *The Baby Consultant*. Sara Orwig offers us a marriage of convenience in *The Cowboy's Seductive Proposal*. Next, experience love on a ranch in *Hart's Baby* by Christy Lockhart. And opposites attract in *The Scandalous Heiress* by Kathryn Taylor.

So, indulge yourself in 1999 with Silhouette Desire—powerful, provocative and passionate love stories that speak to today's multifaceted woman. Each month we offer you six compelling romances to meet your many moods, with heroines you'll care about and heroes to die for. Silhouette Desire is everything *you* desire in a romance novel.

Enjoy!

Joan Marlow Golan
Senior Editor, Silhouette Desire

Please address questions and book requests to:
Silhouette Reader Service
U.S.: 3010 Walden Ave., P.O. Box 1325, Buffalo, NY 14269
Canadian: P.O. Box 609, Fort Erie, Ont. L2A 5X3

THE SCANDALOUS HEIRESS
KATHRYN TAYLOR

SILHOUETTE *Desire*
Published by Silhouette Books
America's Publisher of Contemporary Romance

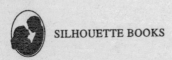

SILHOUETTE BOOKS

ISBN 0-373-76194-5

THE SCANDALOUS HEIRESS

KATHRYN TAYLOR

has a passion for romance novels that began in her late teens and left her with an itch to discover the world. After living in places as culturally diverse as Athens, Greece, and Cairo, Egypt (where she met and married her own romantic hero), she returned to the States, and she and her husband settled in the quiet village of Warwick, New York. Kathryn says, "Although my writing allows my mind to soar in the clouds, I have an energetic eleven-year-old who keeps my feet planted on the ground."

To Debbie Robertson and Melissa Senate
for believing in my story

One

Mikki peered through the crack in the swinging doors. Anxiety caused her already weary body to tense. She wiped her hands against the white apron knotted at her waist and swallowed a nervous sigh. "Are you sure he asked for me?"

Annie tucked a lock of gray hair into her beehive and smiled a toothy grin. "Michelle Finnley from McAfee, Kansas. That's you, child. This is the second time he's been here looking for you."

Mikki's stomach flip-flopped. *Michelle Finnley from McAfee, Kansas.* She glanced again at the man in the last booth. She didn't know much about fashion, but his pin-striped suit hadn't come off the rack at Dandy Don's Suit-O-Rama. He reeked of money the way the diner reeked of hot grease.

What did he want? And how had he traced her from McAfee, population eight hundred including the cows, to New York City? Any ties she'd had to the small town had been buried seven years ago along with the woman she had known as her mother. And Mikki wanted them to remain buried.

"You look like you've seen a ghost, honey." Annie touched Mikki's shoulder. "Do you want me to get rid of him?"

Mikki shook her head. She might as well find out what he wanted before she panicked. For all she knew, the man worked for the IRS and they planned to return some of the money they had extorted from her each April fifteenth. She smoothed her pink uniform over her hips and stepped through the door.

The lunch crowd had thinned to a few couples lingering over coffee. A siren screamed as a police cruiser sped past, raising her pulse and her anxiety level. She stopped in front of the booth and clicked her tongue to get the man's attention.

"I understand you've been asking questions about me." She glanced down at him, trying her best to give the impression of indifference.

"Michelle Finnley?" His resonant voice held the trace of an accent she couldn't identify. Magnificent, slate gray eyes appraised her. He frowned. Apparently she had come up lacking.

"And you are...?"

"Clayton. Clayton Reese." He rose and offered his hand.

She accepted his greeting, noting the solid-gold watch on his wrist. One thing she had learned from her stepfather was how to spot a genuine from a fake. Anything else he had taught her, she was better off forgetting.

"Would you care to sit down?" he asked.

Mikki nodded and slipped into the booth. After a day on her feet, she welcomed the rest. "What can I do for you?"

His pause stretched to an awkward silence. As he searched his briefcase, she had a chance to study him. His angular jaw and chiseled nose gave him a striking appeal, like a marble statue and most likely just as cold. That he felt ill at ease in his surroundings was obvious by the way he clenched the papers in his hands.

"Are you the same Michelle Finnley who was adopted by Sara Finnley?"

Shock waves ran through her. Until her mother's death, she hadn't known she was adopted. Who was this man, and how did he know so much about her? "Why do you want to know?"

"Could you just answer the question?"

"Are you a cop?" One look at his well-tailored suit and she knew the answer. He presented the image of a stuffy, yuppie, corporate type. Maybe a lawyer. She certainly felt as if she was on trial.

"Does the name Megan Hawthorne mean anything to you?" he asked.

Although the name didn't seem to strike a familiar chord, a strangely numbing sensation enveloped her. "Should it?"

He exhaled deeply. "Is that a no?"

She tilted her head to one side. "Tell me something. Is it possible for you to smile while you're doing this?"

"Excuse me?"

"You're asking me a bunch of questions you obviously know the answers to already. If you're doing it for a laugh, you might as well look like you're enjoying it."

Clayton leaned back in the vinyl seat. Beads of perspiration settled around the collar of his starched white shirt. In spite of the stifling summer heat, the woman across from him remained cool. She would probably be pretty if she hadn't pulled her dark hair into a cascading ponytail. Thick black eyeliner framed a pair of large, dark eyes, making her seem older than the twenty-three years he knew her to be.

She wasn't what he had expected. Was it possible that this sassy waitress was Richard's missing daughter? Someone had done their homework, but Michelle Finnley didn't fit his image of a first-rate con artist. Was she working with a partner?

"It's been a long day, Mr. Reese. If you're making a point, I wish you'd get to it."

"All right. Let's say, for the sake of argument, my client is trying to locate his biological daughter."

Her eyes seemed to double in size. An act, or genuine surprise, he wondered.

"And you think that's me?"

"It's possible." He kept his response noncommittal. Until he knew what was going on, he didn't want to divulge too much information. "That's what I'm trying to find out."

"What makes you think I want to know my biological parents?"

He nearly choked on his now-cold coffee. For twenty years Richard had followed every crackpot lead trying to locate his kidnapped daughter. Whoever sent this new information might be playing a cruel hoax on a sick man. Clayton was determined to see that Richard wasn't hurt again.

"Are you going to cooperate or not?"

"I'll think about it. Where can I reach you?" She ran the tip of her tongue across her full lips. If she meant to distract him with the provocative gesture, she almost succeeded.

He had hoped for more information, but he sensed that pushing her would accomplish nothing. Whether she was an innocent pawn or a master player would become evident in due time. He removed a business card from his wallet and wrote down the name of his hotel on the back.

She read the information and let out a whistle. "Nice place."

They rose at the same time. As she passed in front of him, his stare remained riveted to her slim hips, swaying as she walked. His body temperature rose along with his pulse. Suddenly she turned. Unable to stop his gait midstride, he dropped his briefcase and reached out reflexively to grab her tiny waist as they collided. Her hands came up to his chest, grasping the fabric of his jacket.

Their gazes locked. Something akin to emotion constricted his chest, and the rest of his anatomy reacted in an equally uncomfortable manner. Her onyx eyes were beguiling: a paradox of innocence and experience. So, he was wrong. Michelle Finnley was more than pretty. She was beautiful, despite her best efforts to make herself look tough.

Gradually her tight grip loosened. She wriggled out of his embrace and slid her hands shyly into her pockets. "You can breathe now."

Clayton picked up his briefcase. "What?"

"I've touched ice blocks that give off more warmth than you. It was an accident that won't happen again."

She wasn't the first woman to comment on his lack of warmth, but she was the first to provoke such a fire inside him. Far from minding the incidental contact, he had enjoyed the feel of her hands on him far too much. Thankfully she had misread the cause of his tension.

"Is there a pay phone around here?" he asked, anxious to break the embarrassing silence.

"Two blocks down at the pharmacy." She tipped her head and took another step back. "You'll be hearing from me."

Clayton nodded and stepped out into the heavy city air. Although he had made little progress with the evasive Miss Finnley, he had promised to call Richard immediately after the meeting. Then, the sooner he left this area, aptly named Hell's Kitchen, the better.

He tucked his attaché under his arm and strode down the street with a growing sense of uneasiness. How did a young woman survive alone in this neighborhood?

Of the three public phones in front of the pharmacy, only one still had the receiver attached. He reached inside his pocket. Realization hit him with the force of a moving train.

The raven-haired beauty had taken more than his breath away. She had walked off with his wallet.

Clayton returned quickly to the small diner. Michelle was nowhere to be seen. A woman in a similar pink uniform, but two generations older, greeted him at the counter.

"May I help you?"

"Is Miss Finnley still here?" he asked, but he already knew the answer.

"She finished her shift." The woman pulled a coin from her pocket and offered it to him. "She left this for you."

"What is it?"

The laugh lines in her weathered face deepened. "A subway token."

* * *

Mikki ran a brush through her hair and splashed cool water on her face. Leaning against the sink in the ladies' room, she removed the wallet from her pocket and flipped though the contents. A Massachusetts driver's license, assorted business cards and no less than three credit cards—all gold—issued in the name of Clayton Reese.

So, he hadn't lied about his identity. What did he really want? she wondered. He was too rigid and conservative to be a good con man.

She thumbed through the wad of hundred-dollar bills and laughed. It would serve him right if she kept the money, but she wasn't a thief. Not anymore. And never by choice. She tossed the billfold in her purse and quickly changed into her jeans and T-shirt. If she took a cab, she could get to the uptown hotel before Mr. Reese figured out the New York City subway system.

With a soft knock on the door, Annie let Mikki know that he had left. She slipped out through the back exit and hailed a cab.

She had difficulty believing Clayton's story. If her biological parent wanted to find her, why wait until now to make contact? Why not back when she'd turned eighteen and the court records could have been unsealed? Something about his story didn't quite fit. Could his interest lie more in her tainted past than in her uncertain parentage?

Clayton elbowed his way through the revolving door. Inside the lobby he sucked in his first breath of bearable air. His anger had risen with each passing subway stop. How the hell was he supposed to know there was an express train and a local train?

He had to call the hotel manager for a replacement key, an inconvenience that added to his embarrassment. Three messages from Richard didn't help his mood, either. By the time he reached his room, he just wanted a shower to remove the grime. Right after he canceled his credit cards. As he stepped into the suite, he saw his wallet on the writing table. Skeptically he checked the contents.

"It's all there."

Clayton whirled around. Michelle Finnley was leaning against the wall with a grin that seemed to scream, "Sucker." He suppressed the urge to inflict physical damage. "How did you get in?"

"Your pass key was in your wallet." She slid her hands into the pockets of her worn jeans. "You shouldn't walk around the city with that much cash. Anybody could pick your pocket."

"And you shouldn't enter a strange man's hotel suite. It might not be safe."

Her laughter filled the room. "You're not a stranger. I know all about you. Where you work, where you live, who to call in case of an emergency. I even know your social security number. Which is fair, since you seem to know so much about me."

Touché. He dropped his attaché on the desk. The woman had nerve, he'd grant her that. Her lack of fear led him to believe she knew how to take care of herself. Considering the neighborhood she worked in, she would have to.

She made herself at home in a Queen Anne chair. Her silky hair tumbled freely around her shoulders and her oval face had been scrubbed clean of the harsh makeup. She tucked her legs below her in the wide seat. A faded T-shirt, tightly stretched across her chest, outlined the firm breasts beneath.

"Are you going to tell me what this is really about, or are we going to continue to play games with each other?" she asked.

He came to the shocking realization that he wouldn't mind playing games with her. At least not the kind of games that came to his mind. His awareness of her was too intense to be healthy. His purpose was to expose her as another in a long line of frauds. Instead, he was having erotic thoughts about her. "You don't believe in subtlety, do you?"

"You may have time for that, but I don't. And I don't like people coming around where I work and asking questions about me."

"Why? Do you have something to hide, Michelle?"

"Mikki," she corrected. "And we all have something to hide."

He wanted to discover her secrets. Another problem he had to overcome. The situation called for objectivity above all else, and he was fast losing his.

"What do you want to know...Mikki?" The boyish nickname rolled off his tongue with surprising ease. He sat in the chair across from her and met her unwavering stare.

"I find it difficult to believe that a parent who gave me away with no qualms has suddenly decided to renew family ties." Bitterness tinged her voice and angry sparks danced in her eyes.

"Richard Hawthorne didn't give his daughter away. She was kidnapped over twenty years ago."

"Richard Hawthorne? As in Hawthorne Enterprises?"

Suspicion brought an end to his softening thoughts. "So you've heard of him?"

"No. It's on your business card. Or did you think I couldn't read?" Mikki sighed. Her first impression had been right. The man was a cold, distrustful snob.

"Yes, well—" He cleared his throat. "I recently came into some information—"

"From who?"

"I thought you might be able to tell me."

"I have no idea." But she could make an educated guess. Her stomach muscles contracted.

Was her stepfather moving up in the world? Petty cons and picking pockets were one thing. Trying to pass her off as some rich man's missing heir was in a class by itself. A class-A felony. Well, she wanted no part of it. "Obviously there's been a mistake. You can tell Max I'm not playing this one."

"Max?" He drew his eyebrows together in thought. "You mean Maxwell Blake? You wouldn't happen to know where I could find your stepfather, would you?"

"I have no idea," she said, but she noticed the distrust in his narrowed glare. Max wasn't smart enough—or stupid enough—to pull off this kind of scam. Was he? Who else would have anything to gain? *Bright, Mikki. You would.* No wonder Clayton Reese looked down his nose at her. As long as she knew she was innocent, why should she care what he thought of her? For some unfathomable reason, she did.

"I'm sorry you made the trip here for nothing."

"So, you want to call an end to it now?" His question seemed more like an accusation.

Tension gripped her. "Call an end to what?"

"The con. The sting. Whatever you want to call it."

"There is no con." Exasperation raised her voice

several decibels. "At least not on my part. I didn't contact you. You came to me."

"If that's true, you have nothing to lose by seeing it through. I'm asking you to come to Massachusetts for one short weekend and meet Richard Hawthorne. No matter what the outcome, you won't be out anything. All your expenses will be paid."

Mikki came to her feet and crossed the room. Her first instinct was to decline the offer. Apparently someone had gone to a lot of trouble, or she wouldn't be sitting in a first-class hotel room having this conversation with Clayton Reese. She stared out the window at the bustling city traffic. If she left now, he would believe *she* had tried to pull a scam then backed down. One weekend to prove her innocence to him. Would she succeed? Or would she find herself implicated in another of her stepfather's cons without the benefit of juvenile status to keep her from going to jail?

She twisted a lock of hair nervously around her finger. Stay as far away from this situation as you can, she tried to warn herself. But a tiny voice whispered into the part of her brain that still believed in dreams. What if the information Clayton Reese had in his possession was genuine?

What if she could meet her real father?

What if she was a bona fide heiress?

TWO

Clayton instructed the driver to wait in front of the run-down building. Had Mikki given him the wrong address? Broken beer bottles littered the street. An old man huddled against a lamppost, trembling like a lost child. He held out a coffee mug, jingling the change inside.

Clayton paused on the landing and rapped his knuckles against the door. While he waited, he felt the need to constantly check over his shoulder. He expelled an immense sigh of relief when Mikki answered.

"You're early," she said and held the door for him.

"Your house?" he asked.

She shook her head. "It's a boarding house. Or maybe you thought that working at the diner would afford me a suite at the Marquis."

A stab of guilt cut through him. "I apologize."

"No need." She shrugged and led him down the narrow corridor.

Her room, smaller than the size of his closet, contained a twin bed and nightstand. A lightbulb in the ceiling provided the only illumination in the windowless alcove.

One suitcase rested against the wall. "Did you pack everything you own?" he asked, noting the empty closet.

"Better than returning home to find I've been robbed," she replied as if the answer should have been obvious.

He wasn't sure which bothered him more—the dangerous neighborhood she lived in, or the knowledge that everything she owned fitted into one suitcase. Whichever the reason, the knot in the pit of his stomach clenched tighter.

She ran a comb through her hair and checked the mirror. The simple black skirt and cream-colored blouse, although vintage, gave her an air of quiet dignity. She was probably wearing the best outfit she owned, he thought. Could she really be a Hawthorne? There did seem to be a familial resemblance. Or was he merely seeing what he wanted to see for his own reasons?

"We'd better get going if we want to catch the plane," he said.

"Plane? You didn't say anything about a plane." Her olive complexion paled to white.

"Why, is there a problem?"

As if to gather her courage, she inhaled deeply. "No. Of course not."

But Clayton didn't believe her for one moment.

* * *

Only when she was settled in the car outside Logan International Airport did Mikki's queasiness subside. She stretched her arms to relieve the tightness. Flying was highly overrated, she decided. She glanced toward her amused traveling companion.

"What's so funny?" she asked.

"She speaks. Oh, speak again, bright angel."

"Big deal. You can quote Shakespeare." Maybe her conversation had been lacking during the short flight, but neither had he been Mr. Eloquent.

"You've never flown before." His voice was pitched as if the very idea were inconceivable.

"Gee, did you just figure that out, Sherlock?"

His grin faded to a frown. "I'm sorry if that sounded condescending."

"It did, and you are." Or perhaps she was overreacting. Nothing he said or did seemed intentional, but Clayton had a way of making her feel defensive by his polished presence.

"Then you'd better learn from a master, because if you turn out to be Richard's daughter, you'll need all the arrogance you can muster to survive in that family."

She arched an eyebrow at the harshness in his tone. "You sound as if you know them well."

"I should. Richard is married to my Aunt Alicia."

Aunt Alicia. Why did that name cause her nerve endings to stand at attention? She closed her eyes, but she couldn't put a face to the distant memory.

"Are you all right?"

"Yeah." She glanced out the window as the car started to move. "I thought you were his lawyer or something."

"I work for him, but I'm not a lawyer."

"Oh," she mumbled and waited for him to elaborate. Silence lingered. "How long a drive do we have?"

"About an hour. Put on your seat belt and enjoy the scenery."

Once they left the city of Boston, there were miles of beautiful scenery to enjoy. Seven years in New York had dimmed her memories of lush green foliage. She thought about Kansas and better times, before her mother married Max. Before.... No! She would not dwell on a past she couldn't change. The wrongs she'd committed had been done to protect the only mother she'd ever known.

How much of her past did Clayton know? Apparently he had been very thorough in his investigation, but juvenile records were sealed. That he had brought her this far meant he couldn't disprove the information he had received.

She felt, rather than saw, his curious stare. His scrutiny unnerved her. She slumped deeper in the soft leather seat and did her best to ignore him. She failed miserably.

Outwardly Clayton was a flawless example of the male species. Tall and lean, he personified every fantasy she'd dared to imagine, and a few she hadn't thought of yet. He had invoked a sexual awakening in her that was better left in a dormant state.

"I'm surprised you haven't asked any questions about your family."

"We haven't established that they are my family," she reminded him. He wasn't convinced. Apparently the very fact that she worked in the diner was a strike against her.

"Well, your coloring is right."

"Only five million people in New York have brown hair and brown eyes."

He shook his head. "It's different. Both William and Joseph have that same shade. Almost but not quite black."

"How lucky for them," she said drily.

"Not really. Judging by Richard, you'll all go completely gray relatively early."

"Are you going to clue me in as to who William and Joseph are, or do you assume I already know?"

His gaze remained on the long road ahead. She noticed a hint of a smirk. "Don't tell me you can't remember your beloved cousins."

Her patience snapped. "I'm not sure which bothers you more—the fact that I might be Richard Hawthorne's daughter or the thought that I'm not. Either way, I'm getting damned tired of your insinuations."

Clayton groaned. She was so close to the truth, he marveled at her perception. He wasn't sure which outcome he wanted more. As a child, he had witnessed the kidnapping of Megan Hawthorne. The memory still haunted him. Twenty years of false leads and outright cons had killed any hope he'd had for a favorable outcome. But twenty years of silently blaming himself had never allowed him to stop trying.

Every detail about Mikki fit. A little too well. Why had some anonymous person come forward now? Granted, anyone who had followed the case could have pieced together enough information to get his attention. That same person had to know that a DNA test would reveal a phony. So, why hadn't he insisted that Mikki submit to one before bringing her to meet Richard?

"Stop," Mikki shouted.

Instinctively he slammed the antilock brakes. His

heart hammered in his chest. He scanned the area, expecting to find something in the road. "What's wrong?"

"Nothing's wrong. I just wanted to stretch my legs." She slipped out of the car before he could stop her.

Mikki sprinted across a baseball field with the exuberance of a child. Although numerous benches lined the local park's trails, she plopped herself down in the middle of center field and turned her face up to the sun.

Once his pulse rate slowed, he stepped outside, too. How odd, he thought. He traveled this road every day and had never noticed the small park before.

He glanced at his watch, then shrugged. What difference would a few more minutes make? He closed the distance between them.

As he drew alongside of Mikki, she cupped her fingers around his ankle, halting his last step. For one moment he was reminded of the way Megan, the toddler, used to latch on to him when he had tried to leave a room. That little imp had been the only member of the Hawthorne family besides Richard who hadn't treated him like a poor, orphaned charity case, and he'd failed them both when it counted.

"Be careful. You almost stepped on a flower," she said.

He shook off the faded memory. Back in the present, the feel of her firm grip on his leg brought another image to mind. More sensual, but equally as disturbing. He willed his body to remain rigid. "What flower? That's a common weed."

She let go of his leg and plucked the yellow cap from the grass, tucking it behind her ear. "It's a dandelion, but then anything common would probably be a weed to you—myself included.''

Common? No, Mikki was unique. She was three miles away from a meeting that might change her life forever, and she preferred to roll around in a field of grass.

"Take a load off your feet, Clayton. Or are you afraid of getting grass stains on your rear end?''

"We're almost there.''

"Am I throwing you off schedule?''

He wouldn't admit now that he had indeed made a schedule. His trip to New York had been treated like any other business trip. Only Mikki wasn't a client or an employee, and he couldn't make her conform to the strict timetable he had set for himself. "We have a few minutes, I suppose."

Amusement flickered in her dark eyes. "Is there too much starch in your collar, or are you always this stuffy?''

He grinned and dropped down on the plush grass next to her. "It comes naturally.''

"I'll bet it does." A soft giggle bubbled over her full lips.

"I guess you're nervous."

She tilted her head to the side. "Is there a reason I should be?''

"I don't know. There's a chance that you are Richard's daughter. How do you feel about that?''

A warm breeze rustled the leaves. She pushed back a strand of hair from her cheek and sighed. "I don't know. I haven't met the man yet.''

"But the idea of being rich must be appealing.''

She arched an eyebrow. "Is that a question or an accusation?''

"Question."

"Are you rich?"

He lifted his shoulders in a casual shrug. "I do all right."

"And is your happiness based on your money?"

"This isn't about me."

"Isn't it?" She wrapped her arms around her bent knees. "Funny. I got the impression that this has everything to do with you. Otherwise, you would have sent a lawyer or private detective to find me instead of coming in person."

Again, he was amazed by her insight. Yes, he had a vested interest in finding Megan Hawthorne and a hell of a lot to lose if she turned out to be a brilliant con artist. Other than Richard, no member of the Hawthorne clan believed Megan was still alive.

"You didn't answer my question," he said.

"I thought it was rhetorical. Anybody who says they've never dreamed of being rich is already rich or a liar. I'm also realistic enough to know that dreams don't come true and I had better not give up my day job."

"And a gem of a job it is." He cursed the thoughtless comment the second the words were out.

"It's honest and I eat for free. And most customers leave tips for the service."

Clayton bowed his head. "I guess that was directed at me."

"You bought me a plane ticket. Put in perspective, it's the biggest tip I ever got for a cup of coffee. However, I wasn't your waitress. Annie was."

He didn't know what to make of her. In the world in which he had grown up, her work would seem a drudgery, yet she had no complaints. "You're a strange woman, Michelle Finnley."

"It's part of my overwhelming charm."

Behind the veil of sarcasm, she had a gentle smile and infectious laughter that inspired trust. She also stirred feelings he'd do well to deny. A con artist was only successful if she gained the confidence of her mark. Her stepfather had a long rap sheet of extortion and fraud, a career he might well have passed on to her. And she had picked his pocket with the light-fingered precision of the Artful Dodger.

"I imagine you can be quite charming when you put your mind to it," he said.

"First, I'd have to find someone susceptible to my charms. I don't think that's you."

He swallowed a cough. She had no idea. Then again, perhaps she did. "Why do you think that?"

"For one thing, you keep people at a distance. You don't like to be touched."

"That's debatable."

She crinkled her nose in exasperation. "I'm not talking about sex."

"Then what's the point?" he said and chuckled.

"That is my point." She blew a wisp of bangs off her forehead with exaggerated frustration. "Every gesture you make has a specific purpose."

He stretched out and propped his head on one hand. "You gathered all that from one meeting?"

"You learn a lot when you wait on people for a living."

"What other things have you learned, Michelle?"

Mikki groaned. Again he had managed to make an innocent question sound like an accusation. Why did she bother trying to hold a serious conversation with him? He didn't trust her. For the sake of her emotional well-being, she wanted to get the meeting with Richard Hawthorne over with and move on.

She stood and wrapped her arms around her waist. "We should get going."

"All right," he agreed, coming to his feet. "Richard is waiting."

Could she expect the same wariness and skepticism from Richard as she had received from Clayton? Her heart thumped against her chest. She had tried not to set unreasonable expectations about her visit, but the part of her spirit that had always refused to accept the realities of the world still hoped for the fairy tale.

The remainder of the trip passed in silence. Her mind reeled with questions, but she didn't voice a single one. She didn't want to be accused of pumping him for information.

Colonial houses with manicured lawns lined the streets of the upper-class neighborhood. She gaped at the homes like a tourist seeing the sights of Beverly Hills. Unlike the pulsing city or quiet farmlands, suburbia had a delicate rhythm all its own. She blinked.

Toughen up, kid. You're getting sappy and sentimental about a place where you will never belong.

Her resolve to block out her surroundings worked until Clayton brought the car to a halt on a dead-end street.

Mikki glanced at the house before her, set high on a hill. A numbness washed over her. Something about the massive Tudor mansion held her entranced. She had dreamed of a castle like this as a child. The only thing missing was the fire-breathing dragon. She glanced at

Clayton. Well, maybe not. Judging by his heated stare, he looked about to breathe fire at any moment.

"What?"

"Rather impressive, isn't it?" he asked, pointing toward the house.

"I guess." She noticed a swimming pool and tennis court off to the side of the estate. "Is it some kind of private resort or a historical monument?"

"Neither."

"Then why did you stop here?"

The wrought iron gate opened before them as if by magic. Then she noted the electronic device in Clayton's hand.

She shook her head. "I don't understand."

"We're here," he said simply.

As he drove up the winding driveway, Mikki could do little more than gape. She felt an overwhelming urge to run. There had to be a mistake.

"Say something, Michelle."

"Holy Jeez, Toto. We're not in Kansas anymore."

Three

Richard rose as Clayton entered the study. For a man who had suffered a heart attack just one month earlier, Richard looked remarkably well. His face flushed with anticipation, and his eagle eyes were clearly searching for some sign of good news.

"I expected you earlier."

Clayton felt the tug of a grin. "She's not a woman to be hurried."

"Where is she now?" Richard asked.

"I had her shown to a room to do whatever it is that women do when they lock themselves in the bathroom."

Richard's hearty chuckle echoed off the solid oak walls. "So, what was your impression of her?"

Clayton lowered himself in a chair across from the mahogany desk. Many of his personal impressions were not of the nature he could share with the man who might be her father. She was sexy, sensual and hypnotically compelling. A man would have to be blind and suffer sense deprivation not to notice her. And despite the impression the family had of him, he was neither blind nor without normal male desires.

Although he knew Richard would expect a full report, discussing Mikki as if she were a business prospectus left Clayton with an odd sensation. Guilt, he presumed, but why? She might be giving an Oscar-winning performance.

"Everything checked out so far," he said.

Richard perked up with premature excitement. "So, is she little Meg?"

Little Meg. Clayton thought of the dark-eyed beauty. Mikki was not the pesky little brat he remembered from childhood, but a striking, complicated woman. "She might not be."

"What are you saying, Clay?"

"Be careful. Don't let your hopes cloud your judgment. This is not the first time."

Richard waved his hand impatiently. "You can't prove she's lying."

"Because she's not claiming anything at all. She might be as innocent as she seems, but that doesn't mean she's Meg," Clayton warned. He would be wise to take his own advice, because he had actually started to believe in the possibility himself.

He poured himself a shot of bourbon from the bar and swallowed the warm, amber liquid. To get through dinner, he would probably want a few more, but unfortunately, he needed to remain clearheaded for the night ahead.

Mikki sat on the edge of the sleigh bed. The last time she had seen a room like this, a customer had left a copy of *House Beautiful* at the diner. Though large and opulent, the room felt like a cage she had been locked in for viewing by the paying public. Restless, she decided to seek out Clayton.

She stepped into the hall. Her shoes clacked against the marble floor as she walked to the staircase. The light fragrance of fresh flowers was a welcome change from the humid smog of the city. At the bottom landing she paused to view a painting. She recognized the name of the artist, but the sterile cubist picture left her cold.

"A little early to be appraising the inventory."

The deep voice, laced with contempt, gave her a start. She whirled around and met the chilling glare of the stranger. "Excuse me?"

He took a menacing step forward, then staggered. The smell of gin assaulted her. "So, Meg..."

"Mikki. And you are?"

A sneer marred his handsome features. "Don't you know?"

"Should I?"

"What? No welcoming kiss for your favorite cousin?"

Not even if he was sober, she thought. So, he was one of the *beloved* cousins Clayton had spoken of earlier. She guessed him to be in his mid-thirties, although his behavior was adolescent. "Joseph?"

He tipped his head. "Right the first time. But then I expect that Clayton has coached you well."

She laughed in spite of her anger. Clayton had been more guarded with his information than a courier holding national security secrets.

"It's nice to see you entertaining our guest, Joseph." Clayton's timely arrival spared her from having to answer the accusation, but she doubted the grilling was over.

Joseph clenched his fingers into tight fists. "If it isn't our esteemed president back from the hunt." His gaze swept over Mikki. "Pick up a little roadkill on the trip?"

She wiped her palms against her linen skirt. "Last time I checked, I was still breathing."

Clayton cupped his hand around her elbow. "He is better without a half bottle of gin in him. However, he prefers life from the bottom of the bottle."

She realized that she was about to learn how slowly twenty-four hours could pass. With only Clayton to count on for support, her dreams were crumbling like stale crackers.

Joseph stumbled away and Clayton shrugged an apology. "I should have warned you."

"Hey, no one will accuse you of failing to show a woman a fun time."

"I'm sure my last few dates would disagree."

"Maybe that's because you didn't bring them home to meet the family."

His fingers tightened perceptibly. "They're not my family."

"I thought your aunt is married to Mr. Hawthorne."

"That's true. But in this family, blood is everything."

No one knew that better than he did. For twelve years he had worked for Hawthorne Enterprises, the last four as president. A position he would lose if Richard's condition worsened. Only a blood relative could inherit the company. If Mikki wasn't the missing heir, William and Joseph would eventually gain control. The thought of those two pampered playboys ruining the business made Clayton ill.

He glanced toward Mikki. Her wide eyes reflected the effects of Joseph's stinging comments. Just because she didn't dress in a thousand-dollar suit or have her hair and nails done weekly, this didn't take away from her natural beauty.

He searched for a compliment that would ease the hurt. "Dinner will be served soon." He groaned inwardly. *That was the extent of his charm and sophistication?* How did this woman turn him into a social idiot?

"My head on a silver platter, no doubt," she muttered.

"No. Rack of lamb, string beans almandine and new potatoes sauteed in sweet butter." Mikki was strictly dessert. Luckily, he had sworn off sweets. Before his wandering thoughts gave him more than a toothache, he led her to the salon. "There's someone I'd like you to meet first."

She paused at the doorway and took a deep breath. After her confrontation with Joseph, he understood her reluctance.

His aunt rose as they entered the room. Her warm smile greeted them. "Clay. And you must be Meg."

"Mikki," he said, with deliberate emphasis, "I'd like you to meet my aunt Alicia."

"No, no. She's Meg. I can tell." Alicia shook her head. His aunt wanted Michelle to be Megan Hawthorne almost as much as Richard. Alicia had never forgiven herself for failing to stop the kidnapping, and the family had never allowed her to forget. As if she could have overtaken two burly men with the help of one scrawny eleven-year-old. "Look at her, Clay. She's only gotten prettier."

Mikki looked to him for a response.

"Yes, she's pretty, I suppose."

"Well, don't choke on the words," she said for Clay's benefit and offered her hand to Alicia. "It's nice to meet you, Mrs. Hawthorne."

"Please call me Alicia. Your father will be down any moment. The doctor told him to slow down, but he wouldn't allow you to greet him in his bedroom like some invalid."

"He hasn't been well?" Mikki asked.

Alicia shot a stern glare at her nephew. "You didn't tell her about her father?"

Clayton shook his head. "The subject never came up. Mikki shows a remarkable lack of curiosity about the Hawthorne family tree."

"You flatter me," Mikki said. "There's nothing remarkable about it. You're not convinced that I belong here. Why should *I* dare to assume I do?"

Alicia smiled sadly. "My Clayton is far too conservative and serious. He thinks everyone has an ulterior motive."

Mikki blew a puff of air, lifting the wisp of bangs on her forehead. "That's not conservatism. It's paranoia."

"Only if I'm wrong," he said.

A moment later Clayton watched in astonishment as Richard made his grand entrance. His slow, shuffling steps implied a frailness that hadn't been evident earlier. For some reason, he seemed to want to appear more weak and helpless than he actually was. Who was this charade for? Mikki, or the rest of the family?

"Hello, Michelle. I'm glad you accepted my invitation." Richard extended his hand in a greeting.

Mikki touched him lightly, as if afraid of hurting him. "Thank you."

"I trust the plane ride was uneventful."

Clayton couldn't stop the grin twitching at the corner of his mouth. From liftoff to landing, the trip had been an ordeal for her.

She glowered at him, then returned her attention to Richard. "It was fine, thank you, sir."

"Please, call me Richard."

A lull in conversation followed. Both Mikki and Richard seemed at a loss for words. They looked relieved when dinner was announced.

A relief that was shortlived once the rest of the Hawthorne clan descended on the dining room.

Mikki nervously twisted the napkin in her lap. A cold supper took on a whole new meaning. The verbal barbs moved around the table faster than the main course. Most were directed at her, coated in syrupy sweetness meant to sound like polite conversation. William and Joseph, flanking her like a pair of granite book ends, launched a subtle attack of patronizing questions apparently trying to trap her into revealing something incriminating.

Through all the carryings on, her glance kept returning to the patriarch at the head of the table. She searched for similarities between them, and she suspected he was doing the same. He hadn't stopped staring at her since their introduction. His drawn face lifted in a smile from time to time. She wondered how Richard Hawthorne would be affected if this did turn out to be some elaborate hoax perpetrated by her stepfather.

"So, Mikki... May I call you Mikki?" Joseph's arrogant grin mocked her.

"Sure, Joey. May I call you Joey?"

William snickered. "Charming, Clayton. Wherever did you find her?"

"In New York," Clayton replied drily.

"The least you could have done is dressed her up a little better before you passed her off on Uncle Richard."

"That's enough, William!" Richard's rigid tone silenced the room.

Conscious of her simple clothing in the presence of all the designer suits surrounding her, Mikki squirmed in her seat.

"Forgive me, Uncle. I just can't stand to see another hustler building up your hopes. After all this family has given him, I'm surprised that Clayton would be a party to it," William said.

Mikki shot a sideways glance toward Clayton. Despite an almost surreal control, his gray eyes sparked with fury. The undercurrent of tension was so thick it could be cut with a knife.

"Michelle is our guest," Richard said. "Show her respect."

Mikki checked her watch. How much longer would this dinner take? Certainly Clayton didn't expect her to spend the night in this house. She'd never thought to ask.

The conversation changed to business, giving her a moment of reprieve and putting Clayton on the receiving end for a while. William and Joseph wore their resentment of Clayton like a banner. The only ray of light was Alicia.

Clayton staunchly defended any hint of a nasty comment directed toward his aunt. Despite their bitterness, the brothers seemed to fear their stepcousin. Unfortunately, that left her as the target for their mudslinging once again.

"So, Mikki. I understand you're a waitress in a diner. That can't pay very much." Joseph's cool politeness masked an accusation.

"It pays the bills."

"But not on a house like this, I'd wager," William chimed in.

"I wouldn't know. Would you?"

Apparently she'd struck a nerve. William's face darkened. He finished his glass of wine and rose unsteadily. "I've had enough of this penniless street urchin."

"Shut up," Clayton growled through clenched teeth.

"No. If she's Meg, I'm the king of England."

"There is no king of England," Mikki said.

"And Megan Hawthorne is dead. Why won't you all just accept that?" William yelled.

Richard, shaking slightly, dropped his fork on his plate. "No. I won't accept that."

"If you're so sure, Uncle, then she shouldn't object to a blood test."

Mikki swallowed hard. "Excuse me?"

"A DNA test." William cocked his eyebrow. "Is there some reason you wouldn't consent to one?"

Although the request shouldn't have been unexpected, a wave of anger washed over her. She tossed her napkin on the table and sprung to her feet. "With all due respect to you and your wife, Mr. Hawthorne, I don't care to know if I am related to this family.''

She turned and walked from the table with all the dignity she could muster. Behind her, the raised voices jumbled together, fading into oblivion as she sprinted out the front door.

Clayton pushed back his chair from the table. "Nice going. Now we'll have to drag this out even longer."

"Oh, what's the difference?" Joseph snapped. "It's not as if she could actually be Meg."

"Do you know something the rest of us don't?"

Joseph looked as if he was about to say something, then shrugged instead. "No."

"I thought not." Clayton nodded an apology to his aunt and Richard, then went after Mikki.

By the time he stepped outside, Mikki was halfway to the main road. He thought she had left the table to make a point, but apparently she had no intention of returning. The crazy woman. She didn't even have her purse. Where did she plan to go?

He started on foot, then decided to take the car. She had removed her shoes to run at a steady pace. His luck with women had been consistent lately, he thought humorlessly. It seemed they couldn't get away fast enough. Although, Mikki was the first to run out in the middle of dinner.

As he pulled the Lexus onto the road, he saw her turn the corner. Great! Old Mrs. Westbrook was getting the show of her life. He ignored the nosy woman and pulled alongside Mikki.

"Get in," he called out the window.

"Get lost," she snapped, and continued to walk at a brisk pace.

"Don't make me put you in the car by force.''

"You and what army?"

"Please, Mikki. The neighbors are watching."

She stopped and folded her arms across her chest. "I want my return ticket, and I want to go to the airport."

"The flight isn't until tomorrow."

"I'll sleep in an airport chair." She didn't appear to be open to negotiation.

"All right. Get in."

She opened the door and flopped into the seat with a deep sigh. He pushed the electronic lock and proceeded down the road. After ten minutes of stony silence, she turned toward him. "This isn't the way to the airport."

"I know."

"Stop this car. Now!"

He clasped his hand around her wrist to keep her from grabbing the wheel. "Just relax."

Eyes as dark as midnight glared murderously at him. "You lied."

"I said I would take you to the airport, and I will. Tomorrow."

"This is kidnapping."

"There's a phone in the glove compartment. Call the police."

"I can't. You're holding my hand."

He released his grip. What was he doing? He had never taken a woman to his house before, let alone lie, threaten and kidnap one to get her there. Was he having his midlife crisis early? She inspired him to do things so out of character, he didn't recognize himself.

With a moan of displeasure, she settled into the bucket seat and rested her head against the window.

Her fingers clenched into tight fists. Could he blame her for being furious?

The Hawthorne brothers had behaved true to form throughout dinner. Only Mikki failed to react as expected. How could he bring up the subject of a blood test now? He would consider himself lucky if she consented to meet with Richard again before returning to New York.

"Are you hungry?" he asked.

Silence.

"You didn't eat much at dinner."

Silence and a vicious scowl.

"Was it the food or the company?"

Her answer was a most unladylike gesture and one he probably deserved.

"I'm sorry," he said.

"You knew that would happen." Her gaze held his in accusation.

He looked away and shrugged ruefully. "I had an idea it might."

"But my feelings didn't matter, did they?"

"That's not true. I didn't think you would care." She recoiled. He was sinking deeper with each word. "I mean..."

"I know what you mean, Clayton." She uttered his name with distaste. "A *penniless street urchin* like me would put up with anything to get her hands on a chunk of the Hawthorne fortune."

He shook his head in adamant denial. "No! I meant that I've been ignoring their bad manners for so long, I just assumed you would, too."

She arched her eyebrow skeptically. "I must be getting soft. You almost sounded sincere that time."

Clayton gave his full attention to the road ahead. She

was soft, all right, and in all the right places. The thought made him anything but soft. He wasn't having a midlife crisis. He was reverting to the adolescent days of raging hormones, a realization that chipped at his control and made him anything but happy.

Four

Mikki blinked her eyes and cursed her own foolishness. Despite popular belief, dreams weren't free. They exacted an emotional price far greater than she could afford to pay.

Pain seared through her. Even her stepfather, at his lying, thieving worst, had shown her more respect than Joseph or William. Not that Clayton had fared any better, but he had known what to expect.

She shivered. He glanced at her, then switched off the air-conditioning. She was surprised he had noticed her reaction. Working in the diner, she had met all kinds, but none like him. As starched as Chinese laundry, he could be the poster boy for the ultraconservative party. Was he that uptight in bed?

Mikki jerked her head up. *Where had that come from?*

"Where had what come from?" he asked.

When she realized she had spoken the words aloud, she felt her cheeks flush hot. She was indulging in fantasies about his sex life when she was flaming mad. Lord help her if she ever started to like the man.

"Are you all right?" he asked. "You look a bit warm."

She pulled the fabric of her blouse away from her skin. "Perhaps you could put the air-conditioning back on." She would rather freeze than admit the truth.

"We're almost there."

"Where?"

He didn't answer, and she wouldn't ask again. Without her suitcase or purse she was at his mercy.

As the sun was setting, he pulled the car into the entrance of Lionshead Condominiums. The sprawling complex of luxury townhouses was silhouetted against the purple and red sky.

"You live here?" she asked.

"Yes. What did you expect?"

"I thought you'd drop me off at a Motel 8."

"A what?" His voice pitched.

"A Motel 8. The Ritz Carlton of the economically challenged."

"Economically challenged?"

"The politically correct term for people who live near poverty level. It sounds more delicate so people don't have to think about children going to bed hungry at night."

He stopped the car across from one of the units. His eyes narrowed sorrowfully. "Is that what your childhood was like?"

"No. We always had a place to live and my step-father was adept at finding 'alternative shopping' methods." At least he used to be. How had he managed

without his underage stepdaughter doing the dirty work
for him? Would he really be foolish enough to perpe-
trate a fraud when a simple blood test would blow his
scam? Max had never been a stupid man.

"It sounds like a poor environment to grow up in,"
Clayton noted.

"Things could have been worse."

"I guess," he muttered.

"But you couldn't imagine how, right?"

He removed the keys from the ignition. As he struggled for words, she felt guilty for placing the blame on
him. He wasn't responsible for the path her life had
taken.

"That wasn't fair." She touched his arm, and he
tensed. Releasing him quickly, she mumbled, "Sorry."

He nodded sharply. "That's all right."

Was it her touch, or would he have the same reaction
to any physical contact? Although his affection for his
aunt had been evident, he hadn't offered her a hug or
kiss on the cheek when he had greeted her earlier. He
was a complicated man and Mikki didn't have enough
time to figure him out.

A swirl of hot air surrounded her as she slipped from
the car. The smell of the sea hung on the breeze. She
licked her lips and tasted the salt. "How far is the
ocean?"

He drew his eyebrows together. "Ocean? You mean
the bay? You can see it from the deck upstairs."

"No wonder you prefer to live here."

Bitterness tinged his rich laughter. "The view had
nothing to do with it."

She recalled the scene at dinner. "I'm sure it
didn't."

"Let me get your suitcase."

A man of intense mystery when it came to his feelings, he shied away from any conversation that centered on him. Why was he so guarded? Why did she care? Tomorrow he would drop her off at the airport and that would be the end of their involvement.

Unless she turned out to be Richard's daughter. All she had to do was let a doctor poke her vein, and if the results were positive her acceptance was guaranteed. If not, at least she would know. So, why had she walked out at the mere suggestion?

Because either outcome would shatter the fragile sense of peace she had only recently been able to feel. The years after her mother's death had left her confused and afraid, constantly looking over her shoulder for her stepfather. She had fought hard to maintain her freedom. And now she felt the haunting chains of her past reaching out to imprison her again.

"This way, Mikki." Clayton pointed toward the garage which opened with a tap to the remote in his hand. She followed him inside. "I'll put the car in later."

The spacious town house used the waterfront view to full advantage. French doors in the living room led to a deck overlooking the bay. The water had taken on a deep shade of sea green as the last of the sun disappeared. The cathedral ceilings with inlaid skylights made her feel as if she could reach up and touch the full moon overhead.

His home seemed in contrast to his personality. The plush sectional sofa, in beige Haitian cotton, was accented beautifully with throws and pillows in a southwestern motif. The framed pictures and handcrafted collectibles displayed throughout the room were a departure from the stuffy image he fostered.

Clayton put her suitcase inside the door of a guest

room. "I'll make some coffee. You can change if you'd like."

"Thanks."

Once he left, she sprawled across the queen-size bed and traced the Navajo pattern of the quilt with her fingertip. Sleeping alone in this big bed seemed such a waste. Her thoughts went to her reluctant host, and her pulse accelerated. At this rate her vivid imagination would land her in serious trouble.

It must be the stress, she decided as she changed into a short-sleeved sweatshirt and a pair of leggings. Clayton had not made one comment or gesture that led her to believe he might be interested. To the contrary, he kept a distinct distance between them. Even though he had brought her here, she sensed his discomfort with the arrangement.

Mikki was about to search out Clayton when an old photograph captured her attention. She lifted the antique silver frame from the dresser for closer inspection. A small child sitting atop a pony waved for the photographer. A boy stuck his tongue out and held two fingers above the little girl's head. Though they looked nothing alike, they behaved like siblings. She brushed her thumb over the glass. Why did the picture seem familiar?

"That's Meg." Clayton's voice gave her a start. She turned to find him watching her with an odd expression. "My aunt uses this room when she visits. It's one of her last pictures of you."

"Me?"

He frowned. "Meg. One of the last pictures of Meg, taken on her third birthday. She got that pony from Richard."

"And who's the comedian with his tongue hanging out, holding rabbit ears over her head?"

"Take a guess."

She smiled. "I don't believe you ever had a sense of humor."

"I didn't. I was green with envy when you got that damned pony." She noticed something troubling flicker in his eyes. A searing pain buried beneath layers of ice.

"You mean when Meg got the pony." A tight knot twisted her insides. She returned the picture to the dresser. Some memories were better left in the past. "It's very kind of you to let me stay in your home. I'll be so quiet, you'll hardly know I'm here."

Clayton shook his head. As if he were likely to forget. Her wide, expressive eyes would haunt his dreams tonight. Not once, but twice he had referred to her as Meg. A psychiatrist would have a field day with his Freudian slips.

He tried to convince himself that Richard's adamance was responsible for his slip of the tongue. After one meeting, Richard was ready to call a press conference and announce the return of his kidnapped daughter. Only by convincing him that Mikki might not welcome the publicity had Clayton been able to calm the older man.

"So, where's that coffee you promised me?"

"In the kitchen." He waited for her to pass in front of him, then followed at a discreet distance. Her full curves were evident despite the oversize shirt she wore.

"That's some view you have," she said.

"It sure is," he mumbled under his breath. Her legs moved in graceful strides. Long legs that he imagined entangled with his. His body reacted to the erotic image.

Where had that come from? Mikki was either a clever con artist or Richard Hawthorne's daughter. Either way, she was off limits to him. Damn. He needed a cold shower and a stiff drink.

"Have a seat in the living room. I'll bring the coffee," he said.

"That's a switch. Someone serving me."

"Cream and sugar?"

"Black. I'm a woman of simple tastes."

That was the only thing simple about her. She curled up in the corner of the sofa and stared out at the darkness. He had never found anything particularly fascinating about the area in which he lived. What did she see that held her spellbound?

He brought the tray into the living room and placed it on the table. She reached for a cup of the steaming brew and blew on the top before taking a sip.

"Not bad, for an amateur," she said.

He tasted his own. She had been kind. It was awful. Someday he might actually figure out how to use that coffee machine. "Tomorrow I'll let you make it."

She conspicuously avoided his gaze. "What time is my flight home?"

"Richard wants to see you again."

"I'm not going back to that house." Her soft voice trembled with emotion. She was more hurt than he had realized.

"He'll come here after breakfast."

She lifted her shoulders in an indifferent shrug. "Whatever."

"You didn't care for the family, did you?"

"Your aunt was nice. I didn't get much chance to

talk to Richard. The rest?'' She wrinkled her nose in distaste.

"Yes, well, they're..." He searched for the right words to describe the people who might be her family.

"Rude? Nasty?" she finished for him.

"Suspicious."

"Why? I haven't asked for anything."

"This isn't the first time Richard has built up his hopes only to have them dashed. It takes a toll on a family, even when they're strong people."

"Which the Hawthorne brothers aren't?"

Clayton raised his shoulders. "William is weak. Joseph wouldn't be too bad if he'd stop drinking. He's a smart man who lived in the shadow of a successful uncle and an alcoholic father."

"That's too bad. Where's his father now?"

"He died a couple of months ago. Afterward, his mother went into a rest home, unable to shake off the depression that followed the death of her husband."

"Oh. I'm sorry." Her softly spoken apology rang with sincerity.

Clayton glanced at Mikki. Did he notice a striking resemblance to Richard, or were his eyes playing tricks on him?

She wiped the back of her hand across her mouth. "What? Did I spill something?"

"No."

"Why are you staring at me?" She tucked her hair behind her ear and twisted her fingers together in her lap.

"Aren't you used to men looking at you?"

She sighed. "Not unless they're snapping their fingers and asking for another cup of java."

He chuckled. "Well, you don't go out of your way to make yourself look attractive at work."

"Hey, you get enough construction workers grabbing your rear end and you wouldn't, either. Nobody considers it sexual harassment to make lewd comments to a waitress."

"Why not try another line of work?"

She tapped her palm against her forehead. "Why didn't I think of that? There must be thousands of high-paying jobs out there for a woman with a high school equivalency diploma and no office skills."

"I was condescending again, huh?" he said with a sheepish grin.

To his surprise, she smiled. "You're getting better. At least you recognized it this time."

Clayton couldn't shake his feelings of guilt. He had grown up with every possible advantage, courtesy of Richard Hawthorne, while Mikki had struggled to keep a roof over her head. He couldn't let her return to New York. Not while there was a chance she was Meg. And maybe even if she wasn't.

She waved a hand in front of his face. "You're staring again."

"Sorry." He lowered his head. "Would you like more coffee?"

"No. If you don't mind, I'd like to go to sleep." She stood and tugged her sweatshirt down over her thighs. "You didn't tell me what time my flight is."

"I know."

Her full pink lips pursed together in a pout. She tapped her bare foot impatiently against the floor. "Are you going to?"

"No. Sleep well." He watched her stomp down the

hall to the guest room. Her hips swayed provocatively to the anger in her step.

His body hardened with acute desire. He longed to call her back, but he wanted more than company and conversation, the only two things she was likely to give him.

He turned on the television and spent the next hour channel surfing, unable to find anything to distract him from the unrelenting hunger. For the first time in a long time, he didn't enjoy his solitude.

Mikki's internal clock woke her at five in the morning, only today she didn't have to be at the diner for the breakfast shift. A soft rumble of the central air-conditioning was the only sound in the town house. She scurried down the hall to put on a pot of coffee before Clayton made another pitiful attempt.

She smiled. The man looked good; he didn't have to know how to cook, too.

Although curious to explore the rest of the rooms, her innate respect of Clayton's privacy stopped her from looking unless invited to do so. Instead, she decided to make the most of the summer morning and enjoy the sunrise. With a mug of coffee in hand, she pushed open the sliding glass door and stepped onto the deck. Seagulls hovered over the beach, scavenging for the seafood feast that had washed ashore during the night. As she walked toward the bay, the birds took flight to a spot farther along the shore.

With the exception of one hearty jogger, Mikki had the beach to herself. She found peace in the rolling whisper of the waves. Even a seat in the wet sand couldn't ruin her enjoyment of the natural beauty she would soon have to leave.

* * *

An annoying phone call woke Clayton at an indecent hour of the morning. He'd had trouble falling asleep the night before. Not since high school had thoughts of a woman disrupted his sleep. He had spent half the night sifting through old reports of the kidnapping, searching for anything he might have missed the many times he had read them before. As one of the only two witnesses, he had to rely on the memory of the frightened eleven-year-old child he had been.

He stumbled from bed into the shower. Out of habit, he dressed in a lightweight wool suit. As he entered the kitchen, he smelled the aroma of fresh coffee. Apparently Mikki was up, but where had she gone? A glance out the window answered his question.

If he planned to get some breakfast before Richard and his aunt arrived, he would have to go get her. As he stepped off the deck, his shoes sank in the sand. Damp grains clung to the bottom of his pants. He couldn't believe Mikki was crawling around in this mess and seeming to enjoy it.

With a coffee mug resting by her knees, she picked through the bits of broken shells that cluttered the shoreline. Her hair, pulled high in a ponytail, swung across her shoulders as she worked with childlike tenacity.

"Mikki?"

She looked up from her task. A grin spread across her face. "You're a bit overdressed, don't you think?"

"How long have you been here?"

"What time is it?"

"Seven-thirty."

"About two hours." She stood and offered him what appeared to be a shell.

Six tiny legs wiggled against his palm. With a shake of his wrist, he tossed the shell into the sand. "What is that?"

"A hermit crab." She laughed at his grimace. "I thought you might want a soul mate."

"I prefer my crab to be of the Alaskan King variety, served on a plate with drawn butter."

Fingering the fabric of his jacket, she said, "I would expect nothing less from a man who roams the beach in a wool suit and leather shoes. I guess you don't want the little guy?"

He glanced at the small crustacean hiding deep inside his borrowed house. "He doesn't appear to want me, either."

She shrugged and slipped her hands into the pockets of her cutoffs. "There's no accounting for taste."

"His or mine?"

"Both."

Clayton expelled a deep sigh. Dandelion flowers and hermit crab pets. Buried beneath her tough exterior was the real Michelle—a wide-eyed optimist who found beauty in the things most people ignored. At this moment she seemed far more dangerous than a gold-digging schemer out to steal the Hawthorne fortune. If he wasn't careful, she might just steal his heart.

Five

Alicia handed Clayton a bakery box and started a fresh pot of coffee. "I wasn't sure if you remembered that some people eat in the morning."

He swallowed a chuckle. If he hadn't known before taking Mikki to breakfast, he did now. The all-you-can-eat pancake special hadn't made a profit on her. He suspected that only his embarrassment had stopped her from asking for a fourth helping.

Richard came into the kitchen, looking more spry than he had in years. "Where's Meg?"

"She's taking a shower. And you should try to call her Mikki or Michelle." Clayton recalled his own slips and her peculiar reaction.

Richard expressed his annoyance with a grunt.

Alicia touched her husband's arm. "He's right. You both messed up yesterday by bringing her to the house like that and throwing her to the wolves."

"You don't understand," Richard began, but his wife cut him off.

"I do. But we've had twenty years to prepare for this. She's had forty-eight hours to get used to the idea. And as much as I love my nephew, he does lack sensitivity."

"Thank you," Clayton said.

"That wasn't a compliment, dear."

"Really? I thought it was one of my finer qualities." He opened the bakery box and put the coffee cake on a plate. "Anyway, that's not the point. After William's insensitive outburst, I doubt she will consent to a blood test right now."

"I don't care," Richard said. "I know she's Meg. I feel it inside."

Clayton raised an eyebrow. "That's fine, but your gut instinct won't hold up in court."

"So, you're convinced she's Meg, too."

What could he say? His instincts about Mikki weren't to be trusted. "It's too soon to tell."

"Well, I'll have to keep her here until we know for sure," Richard announced as if she could be told what to do. The rest of his family was content to sponge off a trust fund, but Mikki wasn't like the rest.

All conversation ceased as Mikki entered the living room. Her uncertain smile faltered when she saw Richard. "Are you supposed to be drinking coffee?"

"You tell him," Alicia said. "He doesn't listen to me or his doctors."

"Two women fussing over me. Makes me want to misbehave just for the attention," Richard said.

Mikki giggled. "Is he always incorrigible?"

"It seems to be a habit he acquired very recently," Clayton muttered drolly. "Have a seat."

She twisted her fingers together. "I've finished packing. What time is my flight?"

Richard shook his head from side to side. "You can't leave."

"I have to be back at work tomorrow."

Clayton waved his arm to cut off the older man.

Richard would not be stopped. "You can work here. I'm sure there is a position for you in the company. Right, Clay?"

The direct order left Clayton momentarily speechless. Her presence at the office would be the ideal way to keep an eye on her. He wanted her to remain in Massachusetts. So why did he get the feeling this was all going to blow up in his face? "I'm sure we can always use help. Especially during the summer."

"That's very kind of you. But I can't accept." Mikki's guarded expression gave nothing away, but sparks of anger flashed in her eyes.

"Why not?" Richard asked. "It has to be better than where you are now."

"I just can't."

Clayton couldn't imagine what was going through her mind as she stepped outside to the deck. Richard's lack of tact didn't change the fact that her life in New York left something to be desired. She should be happy instead of looking as if she'd lost her best friend.

"Nice going, boys," Alicia scolded. "How far do you think you'll get treating her like a child?"

"We didn't," Richard protested.

Clayton exhaled deeply. "Yes, we did." Both he and Richard had expected her to idly stand by while they took over her life.

"I'll speak to her," Alicia said. "She might listen to another woman."

* * *

Mikki stared at the turquoise water. The bizarre road she was on had certainly taken another strange turn. For one brief moment, she envied Clayton his rigid, orderly life. Her adult existence had been a succession of temporary jobs and boarding houses.

A pair of heels clacked across the redwood deck. "Mikki?"

"Yes?" She turned and rested against the rail.

Alicia took her hand. "What's wrong?"

"It's a very nice offer, but I don't have any office experience." How could she explain her misgivings to a stranger? Although Alicia was her only ally in the Hawthorne family, Mikki still had trouble talking to her.

"There are many entry-level jobs. And the company offers a tuition program so you can attend college while you work."

Mikki swallowed hard. College was a dream she had all but given up on. "It's too late."

"It's never too late. I only got my business degree five years ago. Clayton talked me into going. He said a woman should always have an education to fall back on, just in case."

"Clayton said that?" Mikki repeated, raising a disbelieving eyebrow. Mr. Macho had expounded the virtues of female empowerment through education? Perhaps there was more to him than she gave him credit for.

"I know that I'm being as selfish in my own way as the rest of them. Richard is not in the best of health. If you go back now, he won't be able to travel often to New York to visit you."

"I might not be his daughter."

"I'm not asking you to delve into questions that you aren't ready to deal with yet. But until you are, don't deny him this time. You might regret it later."

Mikki marveled at how accurately Alicia had pinpointed the cause of her mixed emotions. To believe she might be Richard's daughter, she had to acknowledge that the woman who had raised her all those years had been a party to her kidnapping. "I don't know."

"Why?"

"For one thing, I don't have the proper clothes to wear to an office. We wear uniforms at the diner." It was an excuse, she knew, and a feeble one at that.

"I'm sure Richard—"

"I won't take his money," Mikki said a bit too defensively. Wasn't that what the rest of the family was waiting for her to do?

Alicia's gray eyes softened. "All right. I assume you have some money." Mikki nodded. "Then you buy a few things this week, and next week, when you get paid, you can get a few more pieces."

"Where would I live?"

Alicia waved toward the condo.

"Don't even suggest it to him," Mikki warned her. "I'll find a room on my own. Maybe near a university." Perhaps she could make a go of it here. There was nothing left for her in New York.

"So you'll stay?"

"Are you going to leave me with a choice?"

"I can be tenacious," Alicia said.

"It must run in your family."

"I'll go tell Richard." She smiled and crossed the deck.

"By the way," Mikki said, halting Alicia's retreat,

"you did a lovely job decorating your nephew's home."

"How did you know?"

"A guess." The interior had all the warmth and soft color of the woman herself. Despite the striking resemblance, Clayton and Alicia were exact opposites.

"I spent my childhood in Arizona."

"You'd never know with that New England accent of yours."

"Well, I may have gained an accent, but I never lost my love of Navajo art and furnishings. I had hoped that if the place felt homey, Clay might develop an attachment, but he doesn't seem to notice his surroundings."

"You care for him deeply."

"Yes. I've raised him since his parents died when he was a baby. But sometimes he makes it difficult to get close. You have to be more stubborn than he is."

Mikki nodded but reserved comment. She knew she could be stubborn, but did she want to get close to him?

Probably more than she should.

Clayton walked out onto the deck. Mikki was sitting on the rail with her back resting against a support beam. She glanced toward him, then returned her attention to the water that seemed to hold her in a hypnotic trance.

"You've decided to stay."

"Does that bother you?" she asked.

"No."

Her gaze never wavered from a distant point on the horizon. He sensed a sadness in her that had nothing to do with leaving New York. "Richard put you on the spot about the job. I'll find something on my own."

"Would you rather?"

She jumped down to the deck and drew herself up to her full five and a half feet. "I'm capable of finding my own job."

"I'm sure you are. And if you decide to work for Hawthorne Enterprises, I'm sure you'll work very hard. On the positive side, no man will grab your rear end and make lewd comments if he values his job."

Her mouth curved upward in a provocative smile. "And on the negative side?"

"Joseph and William occasionally work there, too."

"How occasionally?"

His laugh held a trace of bitterness. "When the polo club is closed."

"O...kay." Her ponytail bobbed as she shook her head. "Maybe you can hide me away in a file room or something."

Clayton grinned. Richard wouldn't allow her to be hidden anywhere. "We'll figure that out later. Richard will be here another hour or so. Then my aunt mentioned that you wanted to go shopping." He checked his watch. "How much time do you need? About half an hour?"

"Are you sure you don't want to get your date book and check your schedule?" Her eyes sparkled with mischief.

"Oh, that was a joke. I get it."

"No, Clayton. I don't think you do."

"Then why don't you enlighten me."

"Must everything be planned? Haven't you ever done anything for the hell of it? Just because you want to and for no other reason at all?"

He couldn't think of one thing he had done just for the hell of it. He preferred a rigid routine. Obsessive,

Richard had called him. Too much starch in his collar, Mikki had noted.

She turned to leave. "Forget it. I'll get around town on my own."

Without thinking, he grabbed her wrist and tugged her into his arms. Her eyes, wide and shining, held his startled gaze. A gasp caught in her throat.

He brushed his mouth over her full lips. The taste of salt and spearmint lingered. He paused, expecting some sort of outrage or resistance. Instead, she smiled.

As he lowered his head again, she raised herself onto her toes and met him in an explosive kiss. He held her arms behind her back. Pinned between the rail and his body, she squirmed to free her hands. If she touched him, he would lose control.

When she couldn't twist loose, she found a better way to torment him. Her tongue flicked over his bottom lip, daring him to deepen the kiss. He accepted and plunged into the warm moistness of her welcoming mouth.

The kiss began as a gentle exploration but soon escalated to an insatiable quest. She had sent a wake-up call to a host of dormant desires. It had been a long time since he had drawn such a passionate response from a woman, and even longer since any woman had drawn a response from him.

A seagull screeched overhead, mocking their public display. Slowly, he released her and stepped back. He took a few seconds to catch his breath, then glanced toward Mikki, who seemed to be having the same problem.

She sucked in a large gulp of air and exhaled a sigh. "If you were searching for my tonsils, I had them removed when I was six." Her timely joke was uniquely Mikki.

"You were right. Sometimes you have to do things for the hell of it. Just because you want to and for no other reason."

Her cheeks flushed scarlet. She straightened her T-shirt and took an unsteady step back. "I better go in."

He watched her hasty retreat with a satisfied smile. For once, he had *her* off balance. He wouldn't even contemplate his own loss of equilibrium.

Mikki shook her head and focused on Richard's face. Since returning to her guests, her concentration had been lacking. When she had goaded Clayton into stepping out of his stuffy character and taking a plunge, she had envisioned something less physical.

Now he stood in the corner with a smug grin that seemed to broaden whenever she looked in his direction. She brushed a finger over her mouth. Did he know how much he had affected her? Unless he was brain dead, he would have to know. She had no one to blame but herself. She had taunted him into kissing her.

Had she forgotten everything her stepfather had taught her? Never pick on a more skilled opponent unless you're prepared to lose. Unfortunately, losing to Clayton had felt all too much like winning. She had to find a place to live before she developed an unrequited attachment to the enigmatic loner.

"Meg—Michelle..." Richard stammered over her name. "I'm sorry."

She shrugged. "It doesn't matter."

The lines around his eyes deepened as he smiled weakly. "I know you have a busy week ahead. I thought you might come to dinner next week. If you wanted.''

Like a tow rope, she felt pulled in two directions. She wanted—no, she needed—time with him, but she couldn't deal with the rest of the family just yet.

"She might enjoy a trip up the coast, Richard." Clayton's suggestion was a welcome compromise. She was surprised that he noticed her hesitation, let alone that he took steps to ease it.

"All right. Then it's settled," Richard said. "Clayton will arrange a time to pick you up."

Her eyes widened. "That's not necessary."

Clayton tipped his head and gave her a teasing smile. "Don't worry. I'll pencil you in on the schedule."

Richard's face brightened and she didn't have the heart to refuse. "That's fine."

Alicia touched her husband's arm. "We should be leaving." Richard started to protest. "Mikki has a lot of things to take care of. The sooner she gets settled, the better."

Mikki sighed. Why did she get the feeling she had been outmaneuvered? She had to be stronger, or this family would take over her life. If her years with Max had taught her anything, it was a determination never to let anyone control her life again.

Three *hours* to buy a couple of skirts and blouses! Clayton muttered several choice expletives under his breath. Mikki had spent less time finding a place to live. Her only criterion had been proximity to a bus stop. He didn't understand why she had chosen a rented room over an apartment, but the neighborhood was better than the one she had left.

"You can breathe now, Clayton. I'll be out of your

hair before sunset.'' Amusement danced in the depths of her dark eyes.

"You told the landlady you would move in tomorrow. What do you plan to do tonight?"

She clutched her purchases in her hands and opened the car door. "I'll get a motel room."

"Is there something wrong with the guest room in my house? Or is it the company?"

"I got the impression that my presence disrupts you. You were up half the night."

"That had nothing to do with you," he lied. Judging by the way she peered at him through her thick, dark lashes, she knew he hadn't been honest. "Not directly."

She stepped out of the car and waited for him to unlock the door. "I feel like I should be apologizing for something, but I'm not sure why."

Odd, he thought. He shared that feeling. "It's foolish to waste your money on a motel room. Just stay here."

"And be responsible for your sleep deprivation? I don't think so."

He balled his fingers into fists. She had a way of getting to him, unsettling his controlled nature. "Must everything be an argument with you?"

"I came to Massachusetts against my better judgment, and now I'm staying, also against my better judgment. Doesn't appear that I win too many of my arguments, does it?"

Any woman who could get him to spend three hours in a mall had won a major battle. Why had he prolonged his agony by insisting she spend another night? He had no business getting involved in her life. Instead, he should follow his own advice to Richard and proceed with extreme caution.

Mikki took the steps from the garage to the living room two at a time. Despite his resolve to remain aloof, his attention was diverted by her sensuous form. Her faded jeans molded her hips and thighs like second skin. His thoughts made him uncomfortable in his own skin. Tomorrow she would be out of his home, but his life might never return to normal.

After hanging her new clothing in the closet, Mikki joined him in the kitchen. "I'll cook."

"Can you?" he asked.

"I've covered the grill a few times. I'm a whiz with eggs." She bumped her hip against his leg to move him. The contact sent a jolt through him. "I have to check the fridge."

"We could go out."

"Yeah, we could. But if you had ever worked in a restaurant and saw what goes on in the kitchen, you wouldn't be so anxious to eat out."

As she bent over to check the contents of the lower shelf, he did some checking of his own. Had the air-conditioning stopped working? A vague cliché about the kitchen and heat flashed through his mind. He went to his room to change, preferably into something with more room in the groin area. It was going to be a long, hot night.

Six

Through dinner Mikki managed to steer the conversation away from her past. She wasn't anxious to share humorous anecdotes of adolescence. Just imagining the look of shock on his face as she described the thrill of being fingerprinted or the joy of juvenile court kept her sidestepping his questions. She wasn't proud of that chapter in her life.

Once she loaded the dishwasher, she had little choice but to join him in the living room. "Coffee?" she asked.

"No, thank you. I'd like to talk to you." He patted the area on the sofa next to him.

"More politics?" She arched her eyebrows hopefully.

"No. I heard enough of your tree-hugging, bleeding-heart liberalism through dinner."

She waved her hand and plopped down in the plush

pillows. "You're angry because you lost the argument."

"I didn't lose. I gave up. You're a fanatic." His jaw tightened. "Anyway, I think you kept it up to avoid the real issue."

"And what is the real issue?"

"Why are you, a woman whose mouth runs like a turbocharger when defending the rights of the spotted owl, suddenly so quiet in Richard's presence?"

"Do you think I talk too much?" She laughed at his frustrated hiss. As his gray eyes narrowed, she realized he wasn't amused. "What am I supposed to say to him?"

"Anything at all. He doesn't care."

"To what end? Do you think he wants to hear about life with Mom and Max? Or maybe I should tell him what an accomplished pickpocket I am."

Clayton flinched.

She swallowed a lump in her throat and sighed. "Tell me what I can talk about that won't make him feel guilty or me feel angry about the last twenty years."

"Ask him questions. Don't you have the slightest bit of curiosity about him?"

His arrow hit the bull's-eye with painful accuracy. A war of emotions was using her heart as a battlefield. "Of course I do. Do you think I have no feelings at all?"

"Then why don't you ask?"

She edged back as if the extra few inches would lessen her awareness of him. "Because curiosity breeds suspicion, and I get enough of that from you already."

"What I think shouldn't matter."

But it does matter, she thought. "I didn't ask for

this, whether you believe me or not. So, while they're all trying to turn my world upside down, forgive me if I resist. If I turn out not to be his daughter, they're all going to blame me.''

"Is that what you think?''

"Can you promise me it would be different?''

"No.'' His voice was a husky whisper of regret.

"I didn't think so.'' A cold chill washed over her. She wrapped her arms around her waist and leaned into the sofa. Why had she allowed herself to become involved with this family? Why had she allowed herself to care? While their emotions might be tied to the outcome of a blood test, hers were not.

Clayton pulled a light blanket across Mikki and sat on the floor in front of the sofa. After an hour of restless tossing during the evening news, the peace of sleep had overtaken her.

What had he done? When he had tracked her down in New York, he hadn't considered what he might be doing to her life. She simply hadn't mattered. At the time he had been sure she was another in a long line of false hopes.

Silky strands of dark hair fell across her cheek as she turned her head. The bridge of her nose arched to an upturned tip in a feminine version of the Hawthorne men. If she really was Meg, why had it taken twenty years to find a trace of her?

He raised his hand, hesitated, then brushed the wisps of bangs off her forehead. She wiggled her nose and snuggled deeper into the cushions. Her dangling hand settled on his shoulder. Even in sleep, she sought physical contact. Although he had never been a demonstrative person, he found a disturbing comfort in her touch. His growing feelings for her could be disastrous.

As far back as he could remember, he had always been the outsider, living with but never accepted as part of the Hawthorne family. On a business level, Meg's return would ensure that William and Joseph didn't get control of the company Clayton had helped to strengthen into a competitive powerhouse. More personally, he had hoped that finding her would remove the cloud of suspicion and resentment that had hung over his aunt since that fateful day.

He hadn't counted on his own reaction to Michelle Finnley. The proud, fun-loving woman knew more about the art of living than he could ever hope to learn. How much of her innocent spirit would be crushed under the stifling weight of family pressure?

Clayton shifted uneasily. Why did he have so many doubts? He never second-guessed himself. Clayton Reese took control and never looked back to see who he might have run over in the process.

But ever since Mikki had blazed into his life, he hadn't been acting like his old self.

Not by a long shot.

Mikki switched off the computer terminal. A sense of satisfaction warmed her. She blessed the foresight that had led her to take that course in basic computers at the YMCA. She still had a lot to learn about the company and the accounts, but at least she had managed to give them an honest week of work.

She ran a finger over the envelope that contained her first real paycheck. Working at the diner, she had never been sure how much she would make from week to week. When she saw her first real deductions, she suddenly realized, she might not be so upbeat.

The office quickly emptied, most of her co-workers anxious to get an early start on the summer weekend. Once alone, she pulled out a bus schedule and checked the route from work to the mall, then the boarding house. With proper timing she could be home before dark. Not that it mattered in her current neighborhood, but some habits were hard to break.

Her mind drifted to the residents of the boarding house. Although she was the only one not collecting social security, she enjoyed the company and their stories of a simpler time. Richard had called her twice, but their conversations had been brief because she felt awkward using the landlady's phone.

A soft shuffle along the carpeted floors halted outside her cubicle. She stuffed the schedule back in her purse and straightened her desk. An aroma of familiar aftershave reached her.

"Hello, Clayton."

He stepped inside. "How did you know it was me?"

"I'm psychic...or is that psycho? I'm never sure." She wasn't about to admit that the masculine smell of him caused her pulse to race and her lower abdomen to tingle.

"How was your first week?"

"Fine. It must be polo season."

He laughed. "You're right. Come on, I'll give you a lift home."

"Thanks, but I'm going shopping."

He rolled his eyes. "Again?"

She stood and pushed the chair under the desk. "If you could convince the women here to wear pink and white uniforms, I wouldn't need more clothes."

"All right. I'll drive you to the mall."

Despite her best effort to the contrary, she gave in to a fit of the giggles. "You would rather have root canal than go shopping with me again."

"I said I'd drive you." His rigid stance left no room for argument.

Twenty minutes after they arrived at the mall, she wished she had come alone. A scowl frozen on his face, he followed her from shop to shop. When she found a store holding an early clearance sale, she began an earnest search for a few interchangeable pieces to add to her wardrobe.

"How many things are you going to try on?" he asked on her eighth trip to the fitting room.

"Why don't you go have coffee or something?"

"I'll wait."

"Then have a seat and commiserate with all those bored husbands over there."

"No thanks. Just hurry."

Mikki shot him a nasty glare, but it had no effect. Who had asked him to come? she thought, and not for the first time. His patronizing tone and weary frown took all the joy out of her binge.

She pulled a slinky black teddy off a lingerie rack and held it high in the air. "What do you think of this, Clayton?"

He looked around, mortified. "Put it down."

"Do you think it will make my backside look fat, dear?" she asked in a clear, loud voice.

"Don't answer that, man," a helpful husband warned him. "You can't win."

Clayton wrestled the hanger from her hand.

"I don't think it's your color or size," she noted.

His eyes widened like two Ping-Pong balls. Awkwardly, he flung the silky garment back on a rack. "Are you almost done?"

"I guess." She picked through the skirts and blouses she had tried on, choosing the three that would give her the most wear. "Okay."

"That's it?" he asked.

"Yes. Why?"

"Nothing else fit?"

"They all fit. These are my favorites." She gave a second glance to the teal-colored blouse before discarding it in favor of a pale blue one. "I'm done for now. Next week I can come back—without you."

Clayton muttered an oath and grabbed all the clothes from the back of the fitting room door.

"What are you doing?"

With a shrug, he stepped past her and strode to the register. "Shopping isn't a part-time job. If you need them, buy them now."

"I can't afford them right now." That he made her say the words cut deep, but not nearly as deep as watching him pull out a gold credit card to pay for her clothing.

She took her three garments to another register and paid cash. He waited for her outside the shop with a large shopping bag tucked under his arm.

"Would you like to get something to eat?" he asked cheerfully. The man was more dense than lead.

"Go to hell." She left him standing with his jaw hanging open and sprinted to the car.

During the ride back to the boarding house, Clayton tried to engage Mikki in conversation. She ignored his every overture. What was her problem? He was the one who should be angry after the way she had embarrassed him in the store.

"You're behaving like a child."

With a frustrated groan she switched on the radio. Screeching rock music boomed from all four speakers. She used the dashboard as a snare drum and began singing an off-key rendition of the pop song. Her silent treatment bothered him more than a shouting match would have. A surprise, since he usually preferred to avoid confrontation.

He turned the volume down. "Would you mind telling me what I did?"

She glared at him in disbelief.

"You're upset because I paid for the clothes?"

"Brilliant deduction."

"It's not like I can't afford it. I've spent more on dinner dates."

"I'm not your date and I don't plan to put out at the end of the evening."

"Don't be crude."

She threw her hands up in the air. "Hey, you pick up street urchins, you get street talk. Hang with a better class of people, Clayton, and you won't feel so embarrassed by the way they dress that you have to buy them clothes."

A lone tear streamed down her cheek. She wiped the back of her hand over her face roughly, conveying her anger with him and herself.

He hadn't meant to insult her. "I'm sorry if you took it that way. I was trying to help."

She didn't acknowledge his apology.

He stopped the car in front of her boarding house. As if she couldn't leave fast enough, she bolted from the car.

"Your other package," he called after her.

"You bought 'em, you own 'em. Wear them in good health." She ran up the stone walk and disappeared through the front door without a backward glance.

Women! They were put on this earth to torment men. Someone in the heavens had a twisted sense of humor. He gazed skyward and grumbled. "Are we even yet?"

Waves crashed against the rocks, churning white foam on the water's surface. Mikki pulled her jacket tighter around her body as a north wind whipped her back. Slowly, she negotiated the jagged stones of the jetty to the lighthouse.

"Michelle?" The distant voice sounded hollow on the breeze.

She waved to Alicia and Richard as they started in her direction. "I'm coming back," she yelled before they tried to follow.

When Mikki saw Clayton join them, she slipped on her bright red rhinestone sunglasses. He had shown up this morning at the crack of dawn to take her to breakfast as if their shopping fiasco had never happened. Knowing how he hated to draw the attention of strangers, she deliberately wore the outrageous fashion accessory. While he ate, she munched on a piece of gum and blew bubbles whenever he asked her a question. Eventually he had given up.

Richard expelled a breath of relief when she reached the boardwalk. "You don't have to put your life in jeopardy to avoid me."

"She's not avoiding you," Clayton said, then shot a pointed glance in her direction. "She's punishing me."

"Have you been stepping on toes again, Clay?"

Richard smiled affectionately at Mikki. "Nasty habit. We tried to break him of it. Even tried buying him smaller shoes, but no matter what we do, he still ends up on someone's toes at least once a week."

"The Bigfoot of the Business World, huh?" Despite her best effort to stay angry, she smiled.

"Why don't you take your aunt for coffee," Richard said.

Clayton shook his head. "She just finished a cup."

"Get lost," Richard ordered, with a trace of good humor.

"Don't worry," Mikki said, noting Clayton's hesitation. "I won't push him in the ocean. I'll wait until I have a clear shot at you."

Richard bellowed with laughter. "It reminds me of when you were kids."

Trying to imagine a time when Clayton held any affection for her left a dull ache in her chest. She pushed the sunglasses on top of her head and watched him walk away.

"He's not bad once you get to know him. He took it hard when you were kidnapped, but we were all too wrapped up in our own grief to notice until it was too late."

She smiled sadly. "I might not be your daughter, Richard. I don't want to see you get hurt."

"I don't have any doubts, Meg. You do. Until you're ready to find out, we'll just get to know each other again."

"That's fair enough."

He pointed to a wooden bench. "Shall we?"

"Sure." She sat beside him on the seat and drew comfort from her surroundings.

"How do you like working in the office?"

She was grateful for the neutral subject. "It's fun. I've been checking into the colleges in the area. I might as well take advantage of the tuition program."

He grinned like a proud father. "Business courses?"

"Well, actually, marine biology." She shrugged apologetically. "Is there a problem? Does the program only cover business courses?"

"You study whatever you like. Me, I never cared much for the ocean creatures unless they were on a plate."

"And there won't be many of them left if we don't take better care of our oceans."

"Good." He patted her arm. "You can save the world and let Clayton take care of the business for you when I'm gone."

"You aren't going anywhere soon. That's an act you put on in front of your family."

Richard brushed back a silver lock from his forehead. "You're very perceptive."

"Why?"

"You learn a lot about the people closest to you when they think they might lose you. Unfortunately sometimes you see things you don't want to see."

She knew he was referring to his nephews who hovered over him with patronizing concern. Why did he put up with them?

Richard answered her unspoken question. "I felt I owed my brother at least the effort of making something of those two. Your return has made them edgy. They're beginning to realize that they might have to fend for themselves."

"That has nothing to do with me. I don't want or expect anything regardless of whether or not..."

"You're my daughter?" he finished for her. "I know. But it will do them good to worry about it."

She laughed. He was a sly fox, with the silver hair to prove it. "And Clayton? Are you looking to put the fear of God in him, too?"

Richard shook his head. "No. I know where his loyalties lie. I doubt the company would have survived without him. My heart wasn't in it anymore. And when he comes around, he'll be just as loyal to you."

Loyal? She would be content with a modicum of trust. "You're a closet optimist."

"Time will tell."

How much time did she have? She couldn't delay a blood test indefinitely. If Clayton was going to "come around," it would have to be for Michelle Finnley. Because the alter ego, Meg Hawthorne, might only exist in the heart of Richard and the mind of a clever con artist.

Seven

Mikki rubbed her eyes and tried to focus on the monitor. She had never been so grateful for a week to end. With luck, she could spend Saturday catching up on lost sleep. If her landlady didn't ask her to leave first. Five times in the past week Mikki had received calls in the middle of the night, only to hear a click in her ear when she came to the phone.

The older woman had been sympathetic, but after a while the childish prank had become embarrassing. Why would someone call just to hang up on her? Her unknown caller might get her kicked out of her home, but he would accomplish little else. Weary, she stretched her arms and made an attempt to get her mind back on her job.

The hectic pace of the customer service department suited her. Dealing with customers, some of them in foul moods, was no different from waiting on the diner patrons, except that she had the luxury of sitting down while working.

The phone rang and she slipped on her headphones to take the call. "Hawthorne Enterprises, this is Michelle speaking. How may I be of service?" She wrinkled her nose at the formal greeting all the representatives were expected to use.

"How does it feel to return from the dead?" The deep male voice sounded scratchy and strained.

"Excuse me?" She wondered if she'd heard correctly.

"You never should have come back, Meg."

Her stomach lurched and her heart seemed to stop. "Who is this?"

"Before it's over, you might wish you'd stayed dead," the voice warned.

Mikki pushed a button to disconnect the call. She stared at the phone. A terrifying numbness set in as her heart began to race at triple speed. *Someone's just trying to scare you.* She could only be intimidated if she allowed herself to be.

Taking deep breaths, she tried to get her pulse rate back to normal. Cold sweats caused her to tremble. Her situation had taken yet another complicated turn. Now she had two problems. Who was responsible for her being here, and who wanted to make sure she didn't stay?

She had been safer in New York.

The phone rang and she jumped. Her first instinct was to ignore the call. On the fourth ring a co-worker glanced at her, and she had no choice but to answer the phone. She felt a small sense of relief when a customer returned her greeting, but a cloud of apprehension shadowed the rest of her day. By four-thirty she was anxious to leave, when she got another call requesting a meeting with the office manager.

Mikki wiped her palms against her skirt and exhaled slowly. How badly could she have messed up in the three days she had been allowed to solo on the phones with the customers?

Evelyn Drew, her supervisor, ran the department like a boot camp. Even Clayton rarely went over her head. She had been with the company over thirty years and was second in command to him.

As Mikki reached for the handle of Evelyn's office door, she caught the sympathetic glances of her coworkers. "You wanted to see me?"

Evelyn gestured with her hand. "Come in, Michelle."

When she stepped inside, she saw Clayton standing off to the side. His slate gray suit matched the color of his narrowed eyes. She hadn't spoken to him since their shopping expedition last week. Was he going to fire her for ignoring him?

"Have a seat." He held the chair for her, then positioned himself in front of the desk.

"I guess you know what this is about," Evelyn said.

Mikki shook her head. She was conscious of Clayton's stare although he remained silent.

The older woman folded her hands together on top of the metal desk. "Do you remember when I explained how you might be monitored on the phones from time to time?"

"Am I taking too much time with the customers? I'm only trying to be polite so they won't feel like they're being brushed off."

Clayton shook his head. "This isn't about your

work, which is fine. It's about the phone call you received this morning."

A chill danced a slow waltz along her spine. "Just some prank call. I hung up. That's what I was told to do."

"I think it was more serious than that," Evelyn said directly to Clayton. "He asked for her by name at the switchboard, and the tone of the call was threatening."

"He was a coward hiding behind the anonymity of a phone." Mikki tried to sound more confident than she felt. "It was no big deal."

Clayton met her steady gaze. "Is that the first call you've gotten?"

She hesitated before answering. "I guess."

"I guess?" he repeated impatiently. "What does that mean? Has he called before or hasn't he?"

"I don't know. I mean, someone has called the boarding house a few times, waking the landlady. But when I got to the phone, the person always hung up."

"Since when?"

She didn't answer.

"When, Mikki?"

"Since Sunday night."

"Okay. Evelyn, take her off the phones for a while."

"No!" Mikki said emphatically. Her eyes shone with anger and a hint of pleading. "I've handled bigger jerks before."

Seeing how upset she was, Clayton decided not to argue. "Go close out your computer and meet me in my office in ten minutes."

She nodded sharply and left.

As the door clicked behind her, he turned toward Evelyn. The last thing he needed was "ol' eagle eyes" involved in the Hawthorne domestic matters. At least he could count on her discretion.

"What's going on, Clayton?"

"She's a pretty woman and some twisted bastard is harassing her. I can't fire her for that." He tried for innocence, but he didn't pull it off.

Evelyn shook her head from side to side. "I don't think so. I've worked for Richard for thirty years and I have the memory of an elephant. That man called her Meg. Is she Richard's daughter?"

"Apparently someone is worried that she is," he said more to himself. Why try to scare her away unless the caller was sure of her real identity?

"I can't believe it. After all this time. When will you know for sure?"

"I can't say." There was no law insisting that Mikki submit to a blood test unless she wanted to claim an inheritance.

"I hope for Richard's sake, it's soon," Evelyn said.

For Mikki's sake, as well, Clayton silently added. He returned to his office to formulate a plan. Didn't she understand that she was safer if the truth came out?

What could he do with her in the meantime? He doubted she would go to Richard's house, and Clayton wasn't sure he would want her there. Who had better motives for frightening her off than her cousins? But Richard refused to be convinced of that fact. He was as blind to the truth about his nephews' faults as he had been to accepting the finality of Meg's disappearance. He might have been right on one count, but Clayton wasn't going to gamble with Mikki's life.

With all the force of a twister, Mikki blew into his office. Sparks flashed in her eyes like the crackling fuse of a firecracker about to pop. She folded her arms across her chest. "If you fire me, I'll sue you."

He swallowed a chuckle. "On what grounds?"

"I'll find one."

"Your job is safe, but I'm not sure you are."

"Meaning?"

"Did you recognize the caller's voice by any chance? Could he have been your stepfather?" He knew he was grasping at straws. If Maxwell Blake was involved in any way, why try to scare her away before the payoff?

"The voice was disguised, but I'm pretty sure it wasn't him."

"I'd still feel better if we knew where Mr. Blake was. I have an investigator working on it." He sucked in a large gulp of air and blurted, "Until we know who's behind the calls, I think you should move into my house."

She flopped down in the chair across from his desk. "How do I know it's not you?"

He frowned. The implication stung despite the fact he might feel the same, given the circumstances. "Is there any question in your mind?"

She shook her head. "No. I figure if you wanted to get rid of me, you would tell me to my face—and not bother to sugar coat it, either."

"Then you have to agree, my home is the safest place for you."

"Safe?" She laughed. "After one week you'd kill me yourself. If I didn't kill you first."

How could she joke? Perhaps she didn't believe the calls were a serious threat. He was more cautious. "I'll take the risk. Once we find out who is behind the threats, you can move back to your own place."

"And if we don't? Do we become permanent room-mates? I doubt you could put up with me underfoot for more than a few days."

His fingers gripped the edge of the desk. Underfoot wasn't where he'd like to put her. "I'll survive." No one died from raging hormones.

"I appreciate the offer, Clayton, but I'll pass."

"Mikki…"

"I've made up my mind. I'm not going to change it."

He leaned back in his chair and grinned. A war of wills had begun. She might be stubborn, but he had the distinction of being downright inflexible.

Mikki put her hands on her hips. "One word! If you say one word about this, I'll make shark bait out of you."

Clayton dropped the suitcase inside the guest room door. "I couldn't talk at the office. I couldn't talk in the car. When can I talk to you?"

"When I don't want to kill you for badgering me into this." She leaned against the wall and seethed. She still couldn't believe he had drawn her consent out of an adamant refusal.

"When will that be?"

"Never."

"You're just mad because you lost another argument."

"I didn't lose."

He lifted his shoulders indifferently. "Have it your way. Once you're settled, we can figure out a plan."

"Oh, please. Let's hold off on any plans and schedules until I've had some sleep. I'm liable to agree to another of your insane ideas."

"So it would have been better to let Richard worry himself sick over your safety? Better to wait until your landlady asked you to leave?"

She raised her chin and shot him a haughty glare. "She was very understanding."

He flashed her one of those smug grins that made her teeth rattle. "I noticed that she didn't beg you to stay."

"Oh, stuff it." She was more angry with herself than with him. She had caved in to emotional blackmail, something she hadn't done since before she told her stepfather where to go seven years ago.

"We'll talk in the morning, when your mood has improved. If you wake up in the middle of the night and feel hungry, there are some cold cuts in the refrigerator."

She nodded and closed the door.

What now? Keeping her thoughts off Clayton had been hard enough when she only caught glimpses of him in the office. Living under his roof, sharing meals—how would she keep her body from being in a constant state of arousal? Passionate rage to raging passions—all her emotions became intensified in his presence.

Although she had been tired earlier, a second wind left her restless. She lifted her suitcase onto the bed and started to unpack. Inside the large walk-in closet hung the clothing Clayton had purchased at the mall. Obviously he didn't plan to return them. She would have to pay him back.

She added the price tags and removed the first installment from her wallet. Later they could discuss the matter of her paying rent for the duration of her stay. She stepped into the hall. As she passed the bathroom, she heard the steady beating of the shower. Imagining Clayton without his three-piece suit sent a rush of warmth through her.

She sprinted to the kitchen and left the cash on the counter. On her way back the bathroom door flew open. Clayton stopped dead. Beads of water streamed down the wide expanse of his chest. His chestnut hair, slicked back from his face, glistened under the track lighting. A cloud of steam from behind gave him a godlike quality.

His face reddened as he fumbled with the towel around his waist. "I thought you were sleeping."

She leaned on the door frame and wedged her foot against the opposite side, blocking his exit. "Did you now?"

"Would you mind?"

"No. I don't mind at all."

His discomfort amused her. He was actually shy. She squelched the impish desire to yank the plush white towel from his narrow waist.

"Mikki," he said with a trace of warning.

"Clayton," she returned in the same tone. "Now that we've established who we are, let's talk."

"About what?"

"Whatever pops up."

He glanced down quickly.

She burst out in laughter and placed her hand on his damp chest. "Gotcha."

"You keep doing things like that and something will pop up."

She walked her fingers down the center of his body. "You mean like this?"

His stomach muscles bunched. He covered her hand

with his own. His erratic pulse beat against her fingertips. "I thought you were mad at me."

"I am. This is payback."

"How do you figure?"

She wiggled in closer. "You hate to be touched."

The corners of his mouth lifted in a blatantly seductive grin. "How far are you willing to go to test that theory?"

"I wasn't referring to sex."

His hungry stare appraised her. "You corner me when I'm wearing nothing but a towel and you want me to believe that?"

Clayton caught her waist and turned, pinning her flush against the door frame. Trapped in a web of her own making, her heart began to race. The warm dampness of his chest brushed over her. Her nipples puckered through the cotton fabric of her T-shirt. His hand came up to cover one throbbing breast at the same moment his mouth covered her.

His kiss, erotic in execution and punishing in intensity, rocked her to the core. As he pressed against her, hips to hips, thigh brushing thigh, she felt the evidence of his desire. Liquid heat pooled in her lower abdomen. A low growl vibrated in her chest. This was exactly what she feared would happen when he had asked her to stay—and exactly what she hoped would happen when she had agreed.

As quickly as he'd grabbed her, Clayton released her. The unexpected action left her dazed and confused. Struggling to regain her composure, she looked away.

He caught her chin between his thumb and forefinger, tilting her head back to meet his warning gaze. "I might seem cold to you, but I am, most assuredly, not dead. Remember that the next time you want to play games." He tightened the towel at his waist and walked down the hall to his room.

For a long moment she remained riveted in place. *Cold?* The man was a living, breathing specimen of male virility. She recalled her overheated reaction to his kiss. He might be restrained, but he wasn't cold.

As for playing games, perhaps she had pushed him too far, but then, there was no doubt in her mind she would have followed through. She felt a kinship to Clayton she could neither understand nor explain. She wanted him, in a way she had never wanted any man before. In a way that could hurt her in the end. And she knew, as certainly as she would take her next breath, she would take the risk.

Clayton paced the living room floor. He squinted against the morning sun glaring through the window. Where had Mikki gone? The woman didn't have a shred of common sense. He had already checked the beach. Unless she planned on a long hike, there weren't too many places she could go without a car.

Had he frightened her last evening? He'd meant to. Showing restraint was difficult enough without her flirtatious antics. Unfortunately, his plan had backfired in a big way. Instead of teaching her a lesson, he had learned how susceptible he was to the raven-haired beauty.

He shoved his wallet and keys into the pocket of his tennis shorts and went to look for her. As he stepped out from the garage, the humid air assaulted him. His temper rose as high as the mercury in the thermometer. She could have left a note.

"Hey, Rip Van Winkle. About time you woke up," Mikki called out.

He whirled around to face her. She smiled and waved. Her long legs moved with brisk, purposeful steps as she tugged on the handle of a red wagon.

"Where have you been?" he barked more harshly than he intended.

"You didn't have your morning coffee, right?" She raked her bangs back from her forehead and ran a lingering gaze over him. "Nice legs. I'm glad to see that you own something other than suits. Of course, you look like you should be standing center court at Wimbledon."

"You are obnoxiously chipper this morning." Obviously their altercation yesterday left no residual anger.

Altercation? Now that was a pallid word to describe what they'd shared.

"I'm always happy when I find a bargain."

He glanced in the wagon piled high with Lord knew what. "What is that junk?"

"Junk?" she cried, sounding thoroughly offended. "That is some of the finest camping equipment. A dome tent, two sleeping bags and a backpack to carry it all. The couple up on Serpentine Road were having a garage sale. I don't know—do you think I should have bought the kerosene stove? It's too big to haul around but someday I might own a car."

"You bought used equipment from my neighbors?"

The light in her onyx eyes dimmed. "It beats the heck out of stealing it."

"Whatever for?"

"So that I can go camping. There are many beautiful areas to see in Massachusetts." She tightened her fingers on the handle and walked toward the garage. "I'm sorry if I've embarrassed you with your neighbors but, hey, you should be used to it by now.''

He followed, matching his stride to her smaller steps. ''I didn't say you embarrassed me.''

''You didn't have to. If your nose was any higher in the air, you would get a nose bleed.''

''Are you calling me a snob?''

''If the Gucci fits...''

''I'm not a snob.'' He didn't like being placed in the same category as her stuck-up cousins. He had only meant— What *had* he meant? He hadn't felt embarrassed for himself, but for her. She deserved better. ''And to prove it, I'll go camping with you.''

''You missed the point. I bought this stuff so I could get away from you every now and again.''

''Oh, yeah? Then why did you buy two sleeping bags?''

''Because...'' She cleared her throat.

''I'm waiting.''

''Because it was there?''

Satisfied that he was the reason, he nodded. ''Good. We'll go camping together. Make up an agenda of where you want to go, and I'll make some reservations.''

She exhaled an exasperated moan. ''If you insist on going with me, then we go with my rules. I like wilderness camping. No agenda, no plans, no beeper and no car phone.''

''I can live with that. But I guess the portable TV and the laptop computer are out?''

''If you can't live without your electronic toys for a few days, stay home.''

He closed his hand over hers, holding tightly as she tried to tug free. ''It was a joke, Mikki.''

She shrugged. "Coming from you, it's difficult to tell."

Although her body remained rigid, he noted the tiniest hint of a smile lifting the corners of her full pink lips. What had he set himself up for? He couldn't seem to ignore her in a spacious condo. Did he think he would be able to suppress his desires in the close confines of a tent?

As if she could read his thoughts, she arched one delicate eyebrow and dared him to back out. *If your nose was any higher in the air, you'd get a nose bleed.* The words echoed in his mind. He had no choice but to accept her challenge—and hope to change her perception of him.

Eight

Mikki peered through the tinted glass and watched the city pass her by. She stretched her legs out in the spacious back seat of the limousine and sighed. *Ah, the good life.*

"Are you sure you don't want to stop somewhere for lunch?" Richard asked.

"Do we have to?" She snuggled into the plush seat.

"No, we don't have to." He smiled affectionately. "Clayton tells me you're taking him camping this weekend. Are you sure that's wise?"

"Why?"

"Clayton in the wilderness? Mud, mosquitoes and no room service? I can't quite picture the boy communing with nature."

Boy? He was six foot plus of pure male, and she would have him all to herself for two days. She grinned. "I didn't ask him to come. He insisted."

"He's worried about you. Have you been receiving any more of those crank calls?"

She shook her head. Clayton had played down the incident to Richard rather than admit his suspicions. "They put caller ID on my phone. That pretty much solved the problem."

He poured a glass of sparkling water from the bar and offered it to her. "So, how is your new living arrangement working out?"

"Great. Probably because he's been away on business most of the week."

"You're welcome to stay with us. I've spoken to your cousins about their rude behavior. And I'm sure you've outgrown your jinx."

"My jinx?"

Richard laughed. "You were the most accident-prone child. Got into everything, sometimes with disastrous results. Poor Alicia was afraid to leave you alone with anyone. Something always happened."

"What kind of accidents?"

"Little stuff, mostly. A fall down the stairs, a throw from your pony. But the worst was when you wandered outside and fell into the swimming pool. We never did figure out how you got through the gate. Anyway, my brother David found you and pulled you out."

A knot tightened in her stomach. Although she had no recollection of the incident, her heart raced at double speed. With a houseful of servants and family, how could a small child slip out unnoticed? Was there more than coincidence behind the accidents?

Richard drew his brows together in thought. "It's sad. You survived that, only to be kidnapped a month later. It tore the family apart. I only wish my brother had lived to see your return."

If David Hawthorne had been anything like his sons, he wouldn't have welcomed her the way Richard had. The more she learned, the more curious she became about the events, whether it was her past or not. Perhaps the time had come to take Clayton up on his offer and ask questions. She would have his undivided attention for the next couple of days.

"As much as I hate to leave the comfort and company of this heavenly car, I have to get back to work. My lunch hour is nearly over."

Richard nodded a reluctant agreement. "Perhaps we could do this again. Maybe next time we could even stop for lunch."

She smiled. "I'd like that." She genuinely enjoyed Richard's company. An affection he seemed to return. Would he still feel the same if a blood test failed to prove a family connection?

Clayton steered his car around the obstacle course of potholes lining the narrow road. When he thought of the possible damage to his shocks, he groaned. Would Mikki listen to him? No. He suggested Cape Cod for a first outing; she insisted on the Berkshires. He mentioned that they should wait until morning; she dug in and they left as soon as they had finished dinner.

With the last of the sun about to dip below the horizon, they would be setting up camp in the dark. "You did call ahead to make sure they had room for us, right?" he asked.

"Of course. I rang up Smokey the Bear this morning and told him to hold a spot with a view of the water."

He ignored her joke. "I thought the campground was just down this road."

"Campground? Is that what you understood?" Her

eyes widened innocently. "I meant I wanted to set up camp just ahead."

"Is that permitted?"

"If Ranger Smith tells us to move it, we'll know it isn't."

"What?"

"Jeez, Clayton. Lighten up. Camping is permitted in this area."

He muttered an oath under his breath. She was a torment. Punishment personified for every sin he had ever committed. Although he had insinuated himself on this trip, he suspected she had planned it that way. Not once had she tried to talk him out of accompanying her.

"This looks like a nice spot," she said.

"How can you tell?" He pulled the car off the dirt road between two trees. A clearing seemed to have been cut out.

"There're marked sights. There's even a water hookup and a picnic table."

"All the comforts of home."

She smiled impishly. "You've got me. What else could you want?"

He shot her a disbelieving glare.

"Never mind. Don't answer that. We had better set up quickly."

"You're absolutely sure you don't want to stay at that charming little inn a few miles back?"

She reached for the door handle. "Come on. This will be fun."

Fun? For her, perhaps. She would enjoy his discomfort. He owed her that much. After what she had been through the past two weeks, if this made her happy, then he was willing to make a complete and utter fool of himself.

"Pop the trunk," she called out.

He released the lever and stepped out of the car. She was removing the tent when he joined her. "What do we do first?"

"You mean you don't know, either?"

"Don't tell me you don't know how to set up this contraption."

"Two poles and six stakes. How hard can it be?"

She laughed and unrolled the tight bundle. He held one end taut while she inserted the pole through the loops. The other side took more effort but, in under five minutes, the job was completed. The nylon dome, home for the next two days, stood proudly in the clearing.

Mikki set a battery-operated lantern on the picnic table and sat on the wooden bench. "You've been a really good sport about this."

He straddled the bench next to her. "That's because I plan to sleep in the car. It's got reclining seats, a quad sound system and air-conditioning."

She playfully punched his shoulder. "You wouldn't."

"No. But I might tomorrow. We'll see how this night goes. So, Mother Nature, what do we do for excitement?"

"I brought cards."

"Strip poker?" he asked hopefully.

"You're on."

He waved his hands. "No way. You agreed too easily. You must be a card shark."

"No." A wide grin lit her entire face. "But I'm a hell of a good cheater."

"I'd lose the shirt off my back."

She ran her tongue across her top lip and winked. "I'd be playing for your BVDs."

"You're a shameless flirt."

"Does that bother you?"

"I'm not sure. Do you make a habit of this?"

Her smile faded. "Are you asking me if I've had a lot of men in my life?"

He hadn't done so consciously, but he had to admit, he was curious, and maybe even a shade jealous. He shrugged. "I guess I am. But you don't have to answer."

She blinked slowly and exhaled a sad sigh. "No. The one relationship I did have was enough to make me wary for a long time."

What did he see reflected in the depth of her eyes? Anger or hurt? "What happened?"

Her throaty laughter was tinged with irony. "After he graduated college, I wasn't good enough for him. My family wasn't rich."

"He was a fool."

"Because I might be Richard Hawthorne's daughter?"

"No. Because he lost an incredibly beautiful woman."

She had encountered some nasty situations and had come out swinging, yet the compliment caused her to retreat in awkward silence.

"What's wrong?"

Giving her undivided attention to the frayed edge of her shorts, she mumbled, "I think we should hit the sack early tonight."

"I'm all for that."

Her smile returned. Whatever had been bothering her

had slipped back into the past. "Just make sure your zipper stays fastened."

His jaw dropped a notch. "Do you always assume the worst about men?"

"I was talking about your sleeping bag. What did you think I meant?"

Choking on the foot in his mouth, he grumbled, "I knew that."

"Just so you know, if you feel something slithering in beside you tonight, it won't be me." She rose and skipped toward the tent.

"Well, if you feel something slipping in your sleeping bag, it will be me."

"Promises, promises." She scooted inside.

He chuckled and filled his lungs with pure mountain air. Although he would never spoil Mikki's fun by admitting the truth, he enjoyed the seclusion and peace of the area.

A screech owl broke the silence of the night. He grabbed the lantern and joined her in the tent.

Mikki had changed into an oversize T-shirt that hid little of her delicate curves. Her long legs were folded beneath her as she fumbled through her backpack.

"You're not afraid of a little bird, are you?" she asked with a glint of amusement in her eyes.

"Nope. I'm just anxious to sleep on the ground in a ten-by-ten shoe box so that tomorrow I can hike through poison ivy to pick berries and eat bark off of trees, while hoping I don't spook a skunk or tick off a mother bear. Is this place great or what?" He flopped down on the sleeping bag and groaned.

His monologue sent her into a fit of giggles. "I knew you would like it here." She stretched out alongside him. For a long moment she stared pensively. "Thank you for coming."

In an action that surprised her as much as himself, he caught her around the waist and pulled her closer. "I need you next to me. For protection from that owl."

Foolish move, he discovered. Curled up against him, Mikki apparently had no trouble falling asleep. He wasn't afforded the same luxury. If only he could block out the lilac scent of her hair, close his mind to the silky smoothness of her skin. If he could just forget that she had nothing on beneath her flimsy T-shirt, he might get some sleep himself.

Mikki wrapped a towel around her hair and slipped her feet into a pair of flip-flops. After collecting her shampoo and soap, she sprinted back to the camp site. The mountain air felt heavenly against her damp skin, but her plan to sneak back unnoticed failed.

Clayton had awakened and dressed in the five minutes she had been gone. Arms folded across his chest, he paced the ground between the tent and the table. When he saw her, relief and anger flashed in his eyes.

"Out for a morning swim?"

She looked contrite. "You caught me. There are bathrooms and showers about three hundred yards from here."

"Why didn't you tell me that last night instead of letting me…"

"Commune with nature?" She draped her arms around his neck. "Because it's what you expected and I didn't want to disappoint you."

"Anything else you forgot to tell me?"

"I prefer to let you explore on your own."

He cocked his eyebrow suggestively. Resting his hands on the small of her back, he coaxed her closer with gentle pressure. "Do you care where I begin?"

"Why, Clayton Reese, that is the first halfway suggestive offer you've made me. What did you have in mind?"

The stiff denim of his new jeans brushed against her leg. He smiled at her involuntary tremble. "I thought a long walk through the woods might be nice."

"A walk?" Disappointment brought a frown. "Right now?"

"Call it payback." He released her and took a step back. "I wouldn't want you to think I'm easy."

Easy? There was nothing easy about him. When he had held her in his arms last night, she thought they had made progress. Wishful thinking, she realized. He had held her pinned against his chest so she couldn't touch him. Why wouldn't he allow her to get close?

Clayton stretched out on a blanket in the secluded cove and watched while Mikki swam in a pond. His stomach knotted as she dove from a boulder and disappeared below the surface. She was a strong swimmer, not the three-year-old he remembered, but he couldn't fully relax until she finally emerged from the water.

She shook her head, sending a spray of cool water across his shirt. "How's the fishing going?"

He held up the piece of string with a hook sporting a rubber worm. "You were expecting me to catch Moby Dick with this perhaps."

"Oh well, I guess we'll have to eat bark tonight." She pulled a T-shirt over her bikini. The combed cotton clung to her breasts and flat belly.

Before he could stop her, she sat behind him, snaking her arms and legs around him. He willed his body to ignore the feel of her pressed against his back.

"Would you relax," she whispered.

Relax. He felt as if he would explode. Her fingers kneaded his chest in a slow rhythm while her toes toyed with the bottom of his jeans. "Mikki..."

"Shut up, Clayton. You think too much. Just let things happen."

"You don't understand."

"Well, it's not from lack of trying. Why did you come with me if you planned to keep pushing me away?"

"To keep an eye on you."

"Like you used to with Meg? A big brother-little sister relationship?"

"It's more involved than that." And much more complicated. What he felt for her was far from brotherly. He would never convince her family that pursuing Mikki wasn't a self-serving act. He wasn't too sure himself. Opposites in every way, their only common link was the company he ran—the same one she might own someday soon.

As her breath drifted over his neck, and her hands rubbed circles on his thighs, the reasons he should maintain the status quo faded to the farthest recesses of his mind. "Should we go back to camp?"

"And give you a chance to change your mind? Not on your life."

He wasn't surprised that she would choose to make love in the middle of the forest. Self-conscious, but not surprised. He scanned the landscape looking for signs of life. They seemed to be the only two people in the world. If only that were true.

Nine

Mikki knelt before him. Shining strands of sundried hair framed a face that was flushed with anticipation. Her fingers worked the buttons of his shirt with expert precision. He hadn't noticed until she pushed it off his shoulders.

Although sex was nothing new to him, the desire to satisfy his partner was. Enough to raise his anxiety level. Now would be an appropriate time for his arrogant self-confidence to surface. "I think I should warn you. I've been told I'm better in the boardroom than the bedroom."

"It takes two to have lousy sex. You aren't going to scare me off." She shrugged out of her T-shirt and tossed it aside. Reaching behind, she unsnapped her bikini top. The small slip of lycra fell to the blanket.

Her lack of inhibition might stem from the fact that she had nothing to be shy about. She was more perfect than he'd imagined, and he had thought about this moment often.

He traced his finger over the tan outlining one breast and down to the pink nipple growing taut as his thumb stroked the tip. She arched closer, conveying her pleasure with a sigh.

Lowering his head, he laved the rosy peak with his tongue and sucked with a greedy hunger that shocked him. Her fingers, cupped firmly at the back of his head, urged him to continue. He had neither the desire, nor the willpower to stop. She tasted as fresh and sweet as the mountain water.

A muted moan escaped her lips. He raised his head. Her eyes, glazed with passion, held him entranced. She stroked her trembling hand over the fly of his jeans.

He groaned.

"I guess there are some places you do like to be touched." She popped the snap at his waist and tugged at the zipper. "Take 'em off."

Her husky demand ricocheted through him. "You're a pushy little one, aren't you?" Surprisingly, he didn't feel threatened by her aggressive manner.

"If I waited for you to make the first move, you'd still be trying to catch a fish."

They worked together to remove the remainder of his clothing. Fully naked, he knelt down in front of her. "Umm, Mikki..."

"Need this?" She held out the foil packet that had been in his wallet.

"How did you do that?" he asked in wonder.

"Picking pockets is a talent that occasionally has practical uses. Would you like me to open it for you?"

He chuckled. "No. Allow me to have some control."

Mikki smiled. He had loosened up a bit, but he still had a way to go.

She cupped her hands around his hard shaft. Her sharp intake of breath echoed his own. He was bigger than she expected, an irresistible combination of silky smoothness and iron strength. She quivered, impatient to feel him inside her.

Inching closer, she brushed against him. His musky scent was utterly masculine. A surge of heat burned a path to her lower abdomen where his arousal pressed firmly against her flesh.

"Clayton." Her voice was a whispered plea. It felt as if she had waited so long for him. Had she only known him two weeks, or had it really been twenty years?

He ran his thumb over the strings that held her bikini bottoms in place.

"Rip it," she muttered. When he hesitated, she accomplished the deed herself.

He grinned, looking mighty pleased with himself. "You are out of control."

"You're damn right." The need to connect with him bordered on obsession.

With an unsteady hand on his chest, she urged him back until he was sitting on his heels. He fumbled with the foil packet, as if deliberately taking his time to torment her. When he finally finished, she straddled her legs across his hips.

His hands molded her waist, holding her weight as he pushed inside. Her breath caught in her throat.

"I hurt you," he said apologetically.

She shook her head. "No." More like a case of last-minute jitters.

As he gave her time to relax, he remained motionless. An effort that cost him, if his shallow breathing was anything to judge by. She rocked back and forth, all the tension washing away as her body accommodated him.

She gazed at him through glassy eyes. "You feel good."

"So do you." He met her parted lips in an explosive kiss, plunging his tongue into her mouth, tasting, teasing, arousing her even further.

Mikki caught his hand, guiding his fingers to the thatch of hair between her legs. Clayton marveled at her boldness. She knew what she liked, and she wasn't afraid to show him how to please her.

As he parted the soft fold hidden below, she grasped his shoulders and arched her back. He grazed his knuckle over the sensitive bud at the center. She was hot and wet and trembling under his touch.

Encouraged by her response, he repeated the process several times, each stroke taking her closer to the edge. She was enjoying what he did to her body. Her pleasure gave him a cocky sense of self-satisfaction and relieved any previous anxiety.

He caught the hard peak of her breast playfully in his teeth. She tightened around him, writhing with frenzied abandon. Her movement nearly sent him right over, too.

"I can't wait much longer." His husky voice reflected his need. He held his breath and blinked, hoping to delay the inevitable a few moments longer.

"Then don't." Her words spilled out with a breathless moan.

He lowered her onto the blanket and covered her with the full weight of his body. Setting a rhythm, slowly at first but quickly gaining momentum, he filled her time and time again. She matched his every move. A tangle of arms and legs meshed together in a singular pursuit.

Her unrestrained moans and adorable squeaks and sighs were music. As spasms rocked her body, she cried out his name. The last of his control slipped away. Driving deep inside one last time, he gave in to the long awaited release.

Mikki clung to him. Her warm breath fanned his neck and shoulders as the last of his tremors subsided. He'd known they would make sparks, knew they would generate heat. What he hadn't expected was that making love with her would be so much fun.

In the middle of the forest with Mikki, Clayton felt at home for the first time in his life. He struggled for words, for anything that would convey his emotions, but verbalizing his feelings never came easy.

Eyes as dark and shining as onyx studied him intently. Still panting for a normal breath, her face aglow with contentment, she was the most beautiful woman he had ever known. Generous and giving, and completely trusting. She stroked the back of her hand along his cheek, his shoulder. Then she did the last thing he had expected.

She laughed. Not a soft giggle. A side splitting in-his-face laugh.

"What's so funny?"

"You are."

He rolled off her and onto his back. He rested his arm across his eyes to shield the sun and avoid her amused gaze. Apparently he'd misread her reaction. "Sorry you were disappointed."

"I wasn't. Couldn't you tell, or do you need to have your ego stroked?" She poked a finger in his ribs.

"Better in the boardroom than the bedroom? If that's true, I can't wait to get you naked on that solid oak table."

A wave of relief ran through him. She was a complex woman who kept him off balance. He turned on his side. "My conference table? Is no place sacred?"

"If you're there? Probably not. I like to shock you."

"Well, if we don't get dressed, we might shock some happy campers."

"Not yet." She curled against him, slipping her leg between his. "I like the feel of your skin against mine."

"What is this obsession you have with touching?"

"What is your hang-up with it? To hold. To be held. It's a natural expression of affection."

Or a means to restrain and subdue. He shuddered. An arm across his throat had nearly choked the life out of him. He could only watch helplessly as a sharp blow had sent his aunt tumbling to the ground in a senseless heap. Watch as a thug had grabbed a screaming child and covered her mouth to muffle her cries. Watch two men make a clean getaway with Meg while his young life had fallen apart.

Mikki was the first person in years who could touch him without making his skin crawl. She had the opposite effect. From the moment she had picked his pocket, he had experienced a range of emotions, but none had been unpleasant. Was that because subconsciously he knew she was Meg?

The rustle of leaves and twigs sent him bolting upright. Hastily, he yanked his shirt across Mikki, but she didn't appear to be concerned.

"It's only Bambi and a few of his friends," she said and laughed. "Okay, okay. I get the point. You're not going to feel comfortable until you put those stiff jeans of yours back on.''

While Clayton showered, Mikki quickly set the food out on the table. The contents of the cooler she had packed in dry ice had fared well. After speaking to Alicia, she had gone shopping for Clayton's favorite foods. He had expensive tastes. If he wanted to call it caviar, he could, but she knew the lumpy black stuff was fish eggs. French Brie? What was wrong with good old cheddar cheese? And the pâté de foie gras looked like liverwurst.

She tossed a package of hot dogs in the air and caught them with ease. At least there would be something she liked on the table. The fire in the barbecue pit was almost ready. She tramped around the wooded area, picking through branches to find the perfect roasting stick.

Caught up in the search, she was oblivious to the noises around her. An arm snaked around her waist. A startled cry caught in her throat. Panic surged through her, and her adrenaline began to flow. Without conscious thought she kicked backward. As the arm around her loosened, she pivoted around and landed her fist in a solid mass.

A grunt reverberated in her ear. Her heart still racing, she raised her head and glared at her attacker for a long moment before she could think.

Clayton's eyes, rounded wide in shock, stared back.

"Oh, jeez. I'm sorry."

He sucked in a large gulp of air.

"I'm sorry." She placed a hand tenderly against his chest. "Are you all right? Does it hurt?"

Idiot! she thought. *Who else would be grabbing you*

in the middle of nowhere? Her reflexes were in fine shape, but that only proved that the past few weeks had affected her more than she realized. She couldn't shake an eerie sense of déjà vu. As if she had been reacting to a different, more sinister incident.

"You scared me. I'm really sorry. I know I said that. I tend to babble when I'm embarrassed." Her fingers probed his rib cage. His stomach muscles bunched in response. "Clayton? Can you speak?"

He rubbed his side. "Damn, that's some wicked left hook. Where did you learn that? From Muhammad Ali?"

"You're not mad at me?"

"I should have known better than to sneak up on you like that. Just forget about it. I know I will." He laughed. "In a few weeks when the bruise fades."

"I'm sorry."

"You've said that." He slipped his arms around her and pulled her against his chest. "I'm only surprised that you didn't do it sooner."

She rested her chin on his shoulder and sighed. He had just been assaulted for no logical reason and he was cracking jokes. He'd picked an inappropriate moment to discover his sense of humor. "Don't try to make me feel better."

"Why not? Your cousins would probably applaud you if they knew you'd slugged me. They've been dying to do it for years, but they've never had the nerve to try."

Her body went rigid. For a while she had managed to forget about that terrible twosome, forget a heritage that might or might not be hers. She had even managed to forget that, first and foremost, Clayton's loyalties lay with Hawthorne Enterprises, not her.

She wiggled out of his embrace and took a step back. "I...left a fire burning."

"What's wrong?"

"It's dangerous to leave a fire unattended."

"Mikki," he called after her. She sprinted back to the site without waiting for him.

Mikki poked a wide stick into the fire. Crackling sparks leaped in the air. Her rigid movements and silence led Clayton to believe that she was far more confused by the radical change her life had taken than he had realized.

He sat on the wooden bench. "Do you want to tell me what happened back there?"

"I got scared and landed my fist in your rib cage." She leaned across the table and set out two paper plates.

He ran his hand over the small of her back. "After that?"

"Nothing."

"Something happened. The minute I mentioned your cousins..."

Straightening her shoulders, she turned to face him. "They're not my cousins."

He understood her reservations, but she had to accept the very real probability that she was a member of the Hawthorne family. "They might be."

"Do we have to talk about this now? Can't we enjoy the rest of the weekend?"

"Now who's pushing who away?"

"This is different," she said tightly while trying to back away from him.

He hooked a finger through the belt loop of her cut-offs. "Why?"

"Because it involves more than just the two of us. You want me to believe that Richard is my father. To do that I have to accept that the past twenty years of my life have been a sham." Her eyes shimmered with moisture. "That I did…things to—"

"To what?" he urged softly.

A silver tear streamed down her cheek. "To protect a woman who wasn't my mother, who was involved in my kidnapping and who lied to me all my life. Excuse me if I don't jump at the opportunity."

Clayton grimaced. He had never considered her feelings for the woman she knew as her mother. From what little he learned about Mikki's stepfather, he'd arrogantly assumed her life had been so bad that she would naturally welcome the opportunity to prove herself to be Richard's daughter.

"Maybe Sara Finnley wasn't involved. Maybe she thought she had legally adopted you."

"Then where are the papers? The only thing I have is a social security card and I have no idea how I came to have that. I can't get a driver's license or a passport because I don't have a birth certificate, and I couldn't afford the cost of a lawyer to find out who the hell I am."

All the more reason for her to prove her identity, he thought, but he sensed that this wasn't the time to push her. She still had issues to resolve in her mind. He, too, had had no luck in finding a birth record for Michelle Finnley.

"All right. Your past is a closed subject."

"It's not closed. I'd like to take a look at what you have, if you're not going to take it the wrong way."

"Why would I?"

The corners of her mouth lifted in a sad smile. "I

picked your pocket, invaded your blessed solitude and even knocked the wind out of you. And those were our finer moments.''

He pulled her onto his lap. ''I thought our finer moment was out by the pond this morning.''

''Well, you would.'' She laughed and pushed at his errant hand trying to slip under her shirt. ''Did you ever notice that you only voluntarily touch me when you want to distract me.''

''Is it working?''

''Yes, dammit, you know it is.'' She snuggled against him, subjecting him to her own subtle brand of torment. ''And I'm going to become the biggest pain in the rear end so you'll want to distract me all the time.''

''Become?'' he asked. ''You already are.''

''Ouch.''

''The truth hurts,'' he whispered in her ear.

''Yes it does, Clayton. Sometimes more than the lies.''

Before he could ask her to elaborate, she pressed her mouth against his. Soft and warm, the kiss was a plea for him to distract her. He gladly obliged. Soon she would have to face the truths she had been successfully avoiding. But soon didn't have to be tonight.

Ten

"I don't see the point of involving a lawyer." Richard paced the study, nervously twisting the papers in his hand. "I have her birth certificate. If she wants to get a learner's permit, she can use this."

Clayton loosened the tie around his neck. "It's not legal until you know for sure she's Meg."

"I am sure."

"Then *you* talk to her about a blood test."

Richard slumped into the chair behind the desk. "I would, but I think she's closer to you right now."

Closer physically, but she still shut him out whenever he tried to ask about her past. "I'm not sure that she'll listen. Trust doesn't come easy for her."

"You either, Clay. But you trust her, don't you? You think she's Meg."

"I don't think she's after money."

Clayton wasn't sure they could give her what she

wanted. She needed a resolution that would allow her to reconcile her love for her mother and her developing feelings for her father without betraying either one in the process. No small feat in light of the history.

"That wasn't what I asked."

For reasons he couldn't begin to understand, he was as sure as Richard. "The private investigator located Maxwell Blake, but he's been in Leavenworth for the past two years, so that blows our other theory. So in answer to your question, I'm almost convinced she is Meg."

A frown creased Richard's forehead. "Then why wasn't she found sooner?"

"Because she obviously wasn't kidnapped for ransom."

"Have your investigator run a thorough background check on that woman who raised her. Go back to the day she was born if necessary. That's the only other possibility."

Clayton shook his head. "I think we should hold off on that for a while. Mikki won't thank you if you try to find out now. For good or bad, she knew Sara Finnley as her mother for most of her life. Nothing would be gained by destroying those memories for her."

He wasn't convinced Sara Finnley was the answer, anyway. Although William and Joseph were too young to have been involved, their father wasn't. David Hawthorne had resented his brother's success. Talk among the staff hinted that he had been less than happy when Richard became a father after fifteen years of trying. Had he seen the child as a threat to his own sons' future?

"Sounds like you've gotten to know her better than

I realized. Do you think that's wise?'' Richard's tone was a mix of question and concern.

His perception unnerved Clayton. But the air of disapproval stung. It reminded him that he would never be good enough for this family. ''I have to get back to the office.''

As he reached for the door handle, Richard called to him. ''I only meant that you should be careful with her, Clay. That's an act she puts on. She's not nearly as tough as she would have us believe.''

''I know.'' As if he needed to be reminded of her vulnerabilities. He had seen beneath the mask and lost his soul to the gentle dreamer inside.

Mikki folded the foil around the rest of her sandwich and stuffed it back in the bag. The dreary, rainy day was compounded by the presence of William and Joseph in the office. With a commissary just two floors up she could only assume that Joseph's entry in the break room meant trouble. Thankfully she had been assigned a lunch hour that no one else wanted.

He straddled the chair across from her. His dark hair fell on his forehead, giving him a sinister look. ''Hey, Meg.''

''Mikki.'' She wrinkled her nose distastefully. He smelled like a distillery. ''What do you want?''

''Can't I enjoy the company of my favorite cousin?''

''You're drunk.''

His crooked grin indicated a misplaced pride. ''Not yet.''

''Joseph?'' William strode into the room. He gave her a disinterested glare then turned toward his brother. ''What are you doing here?''

"I'm just having a chat with cousin Meg. Sit down and join us."

Mikki sighed. "My name is Michelle."

"Damn right," William shot back. "And you know it, too. Otherwise you would have had that blood test."

"How do you know she hasn't?" Joseph asked quietly.

"What have you heard?" William's surprised tone reverberated around the room.

Mikki collected the paper bag and her purse from the table. Any more time in their presence and she would bring up what little of her lunch she had managed to eat.

"Well, think about it," Joseph said to his brother. "Why else would Clayton be going after her? She's not exactly the ice queen type he prefers. He must know for sure."

"Excuse me." She stepped around William's bulky frame.

He grabbed her arm, halting her exit. "Clayton's hedging his bets. He'd do anything to keep control of Hawthorne Enterprises."

She wrenched free from William's grip. "Well, from what I've seen, he deserves it more than either of you."

"I'll see him in hell first." William elbowed past her and stormed from the room.

Joseph's bitter laughter grated on her already splintered nerves. "I know he hides it well, but he resents Clay."

"And you don't?" she asked. "I find that difficult to believe."

"Not me. I don't bite the hand that feeds me. And if you are Meg, I'm sure Clayton will be in control for a long time to come."

She leaned against the wall and folded her arms over her chest. "Why don't you try working for a living?"

"Well, I would, but I'm the family screwup, as I'm sure Clayton has told you."

"Actually he told me you were very smart. Too bad you go to such extraordinary lengths to hide it."

Joseph cocked an eyebrow. "Maybe he doesn't know me as well as he thinks he does."

"Or, perhaps, he knows you better than *you* think," she countered easily.

His sad smile reflected years of hurt. "You're too naive to be a Hawthorne, Meg."

Mikki shook her head sadly and left the room. Was it naive to believe all people had some good in them? God, she hoped not.

Clayton tossed his briefcase on the kitchen counter and groaned. Silently he prayed for sun tomorrow. He had always cursed the days the Hawthorne brothers showed up at the office—more so now. Although Mikki had said nothing, he knew she'd had a confrontation with her cousins.

He glanced at his watch. Stubborn and overly proud, she had insisted on taking the bus home rather than ride with him, even though, thanks to William, most people at work knew she was staying with him. Before too many facts became fodder for office gossip, he would have to talk to her about the blood test.

Ten minutes later she waltzed through the door. A smile, brighter than the sun, covered her face. Her skirt and blouse were off before she reached the hall. "You're still in your suit."

"Is that a problem?"

"Yes. You remind me of my boss. He's such a bore.

No sense of humor. Just work, work, work." She darted into the guest room, grabbed a T-shirt and returned. "Well, are you going to change, or do I call you Mr. Reese all evening?"

"Should I hang out in my boxer shorts?"

"It's a start." She loosened the tie around his neck.

"Behave or I'll tie you up with that."

She sighed longingly. "Oh, kinky. I like it."

"Mikki." He stopped her hands as she tried to unbutton his shirt. "We need to talk."

"I know. But we might as well be comfortable while we do it." He gave up and let her undress him. "Relax. This won't hurt a bit."

Pain was the furthest thing from her mind. She had turned the mundane task of taking off clothes into a sensual art. Once she had removed and neatly folded each piece, she pushed him onto the sofa and snuggled herself comfortably in his lap.

"Now that I have you utterly defenseless—" she brushed a kiss over his mouth "—we can talk about me paying some rent while I'm here."

The jolt to his system wasn't caused by the pressure of her body molding against his. Although that in itself was breaking his concentration. "I can't take your money."

"Sure, you can." She nipped at his earlobe. "I hand it to you and you put it in your wallet. It's simple."

He cupped his hand along her face and stared into her dark eyes. "I've never taken money from a woman, and I'm not about to start now."

"How many of them have you lived with?"

"That's not the point."

"Listen, you macho sexist. You'll take the money or I'll move out now." She lowered her gaze and frowned thoughtfully. "There's really no reason for me to stay, anyway. I haven't received any more calls."

His heart lurched. No reason? How about because he wanted her to stay. The thought of her leaving caused his insides to churn. So why couldn't he tell her how he felt?

He'd never had trouble stating his position before. But then, he'd never tried to deal with his emotions before.

"All right. You win. You pay me rent. But then I have to pay you for the things you do here."

He felt the tension melt from her limbs. "Like?"

"You clean. Let's see, that usually costs fifteen dollars an hour—"

"What? I'm in the wrong business."

"You take messages for me—part-time secretary. Watch the house while I'm away on business. Security services. Water the plants—landscaping services. You cook breakfast and dinner."

"With *your* food, so don't forget to figure that in."

"By all means." He pretended to mentally calculate, stroking his finger against her cheek as he added.

"What about making love," she said.

"What about it?"

"I mean, do I pay you for that, or do you pay me?"

He chuckled. "We'll call it a draw. Now, that comes out to two dollars a week in your favor. Do you want it in cash or will you take my check?"

"Clayton." Her voice held a trace of warning. "Don't patronize me."

"I can't ask you for money. Put whatever you want to in a jar in the kitchen, and we can use it for future camping trips."

Mikki suppressed a smile. That was as enthusiastic

a compromise as she was likely to get from him. "Now that we've settled financial matters, what did you want to talk about?"

His fingers tightened perceptibly on her waist. "I understand your cou—you had a run-in with William during lunch today."

She had almost put the incident with the Hawthorne brothers out of her mind. Almost, but Clayton's words had brought it back to the surface. "It's bad enough my phone is monitored more than everyone else's. Is my break time monitored, too?"

"No one is spying on you." His eyes narrowed. "William wasted no time in coming to see me afterward. He thinks you're a fake, looking to get as much as you can from Richard before you're found out."

"Is that what you think?" she asked, unable to keep the hurt from her voice.

"If I thought that, you wouldn't be here."

She felt as if the air had been sucked from her body. "In other words, you only asked me to stay with you because you think I'm Meg."

He shook his head violently and tightened his grip as she tried to squirm out of his lap. "I didn't say that."

"What happens if I'm not Richard's daughter?"

"What do you mean, what happens?"

"I'm hardly worth the effort otherwise."

"What is this about, Mikki?"

With a final twist, she pulled free and sprang to her feet. Pain seared her heart. "This conversation. It's all leading up to me taking a blood test, isn't it?"

Confusion deepened the frown lines around his eyes. "Well, you have to admit, it would simplify your life."

"Yours, too, no doubt."

He folded his arms across his chest. "Would you like to tell me how?"

"You wouldn't have to waste your time sleeping with the wrong woman."

"And just where did you get an idea like that?"

She said nothing. Although she knew she was being unreasonable, her minor insecurities had gotten a major boost from William. In his favor, Clayton hadn't insisted on the blood test before they made love. That might be because he felt he had no influence before.

He tried to reach for her, but she backed away. When he touched her, she couldn't remember to breathe, let alone try to understand something that might affect the core of their relationship.

"You've been listening to your beloved cousins, after all," he said.

"Answer me one question. What happens to the business if Richard dies before Meg is found?"

"Nothing was ever decided. Richard was adamant in his belief that you would be found."

"What happens?"

"His surviving heirs would take over."

"Alicia?"

Clayton shook his head. "She signed a prenuptial agreement when she married Richard."

"You?"

"I'm not family. I'm sure you've figured that out by now."

"That's hardly fair," she muttered more to herself. She could sympathize with his motives, but that didn't ease the hollow ache of anger and fear inside. Anger that she was a pawn in some power struggle and fear that she might have given her heart to a man who didn't return her feelings.

"Do you think that's the only reason I want you to take a blood test?"

"Seeing how you've showered me with so many declarations of undying devotion, I can't see how I made that leap," she sniped.

"So now I'm guilty of what I didn't say. Tell me, is there any way I can win?"

"I'm not a prize to be won. Hell, I might not even be worth having." She stormed to her room with Clayton close on her heels. Grabbing the first pair of shorts she could find, she quickly dressed.

"What are you doing?"

"I'm going for a walk. Do I need your permission?" She shoved her money from the dresser deep inside her pocket.

"Right now?" he asked incredulously. "In the middle of an argument?"

She shrugged and pushed past him. If she stayed, she might say things she would regret. Or worse, she would allow him to distract her. She needed solitude to sort out her feelings.

As she reached for the sliding door, Clayton caught her wrist. "You can't leave."

"You can't stop me." With a sharp tug, she wrenched her hand free and slipped out the door onto the deck. "If you plan to follow me, you might want to put on a pair of pants first."

She didn't catch all of Clayton's expletives as she hopped the rail and sprinted up the beach.

Clayton paced around the condo, angrily kicking anything in his path. Tension seeped from every pore. Why had he devoted all his time and energy toward running a business he would never own for people who didn't appreciate his efforts?

He had no illusions about where he fit in the Hawthorne family. Nowhere. He was an employee, albeit a highly paid one. What a fool he had been! He had actually believed that if he tried hard enough, he would be accepted by these people he had lived with since childhood. Obviously he was wrong. Mikki's father didn't welcome Clayton's relationship with her. Her cousins hoped to drive a wedge between them.

None of that hurt as much as Mikki letting them. He had lived with distrust for most of his adult life, but he didn't think he should have to explain himself to her. How could she believe he only wanted her if she was Richard's daughter?

No wonder he had avoided emotional attachments in the past. They were too damned confusing. One minute she was happily trying to seduce him and the next she was storming up the beach. All because he wanted to make sure she wasn't hurting from William's cruel words.

Mikki was chaos, a riot run amok in the sterile, orderly world he had created for himself. Who wanted that kind of aggravation...?

He did.

Eleven

Mikki had only intended to take a walk to cool off. Two buses later, she ended up in the center of Boston, at Quincy Market. She loved the sounds and smells of the city and the ability to become invisible among the crowds. Feeling guilty for wandering so far, but still too raw to talk with Clayton, she called Alicia.

The delightful aromas of the many food vendors reminded her that she'd left without eating dinner. She paid for two cups of coffee and a large cinnamon roll and brought them back to the table. "I didn't mean for you to meet me here."

Alicia smiled indulgently. She was the only person whose affection was unconditional. Mikki felt as if she had known Alicia all her life. "I wanted to. Did you and Clayton have a disagreement?"

A disagreement? By their very natures, they couldn't agree on the time of day. A disagreement she could have dealt with. The problem was not what they had said, but what they hadn't.

"I'd rather not put you in the middle," Mikki said, but she already had by calling the woman.

"Oh, shoot. I know my nephew. He lacks tact, but not feelings."

"I shouldn't have bothered you. You have your own problems."

"Don't be ridiculous. You're family."

She smiled weakly. "This blood test everyone wants me to take—what happens if I don't pass?"

"You will," Alicia said with unshakable confidence. "I've never been more sure of anything in my life."

"All right. Even if I do, there are things about me that you and Richard don't know."

"Your past is your own," she said. "We have all done the wrong thing for the right reason at some time in our lives."

"I'm not talking about white lies. These are black marks."

"I have a few of those myself."

Mikki doubted Alicia was capable of anything that would warrant a black mark. A few gold stars seemed more appropriate, considering the way her in-laws treated her.

"Why don't I drive you home," Alicia offered.

"I'll take the bus."

"Richard would never forgive me."

"I'm not ready to go home. I thought I'd do a bit of shopping first."

"The stores will be closing soon. Besides, you know you aren't going to feel right until you talk to Clayton."

Mikki wasn't sure she would feel right even after

talking to him. However, she doubted Alicia would let her stay in the city alone. "All right. Just let me finish my cinnamon roll. Are you sure you don't want half?"

"I'm sure, but thank you."

Alicia sipped her coffee while Mikki tried to savor the sweet sticky bun. Normally she had a passion for sweets, but today, the gooey treat tasted flat. She wrapped up the rest for later. "Let's go."

The half-hour ride to the condo did little to calm her nerves. Mikki had virtually ignored Alicia for most of the trip. She smiled apologetically. "You are going to come in, aren't you?"

"No. I think you two should be alone."

"I'd rather have witnesses," Mikki joked.

Alicia touched her hand. "Clayton would never hurt you. You know, he came to see Richard this morning. He wanted the family lawyer to do something about getting a birth record for you so you could get a driver's license."

Mikki was shocked. "He did?"

"Richard told him you already had a birth certificate."

Meg's birth certificate. That was what Clayton had meant about simplifying her life. She hadn't jumped to the wrong conclusion—she had taken a flying leap.

Clayton pulled open the front door. Mikki, standing on the stoop with her hands in her pockets, shrugged and walked inside. He waved to his aunt and waited until the car pulled away.

The three hours she had been gone had done nothing to lift his foul mood. He figured she had gone for a walk up the beach to cool off, not for a bus ride into the city. At least she'd had sense enough to call Alicia.

The little coward didn't have the guts to face him. What had happened to the woman who had nearly laid him out flat only three days ago? Was her refusal to fight a sign of progress or a step backward in their relationship?

Tucking a large manila folder under his arm, he followed Mikki to her room. He knocked on the door.

"Come in." Mikki's voice was barely audible through the door. He entered the dark room and flipped on the light. She was leaning against the wall, gazing at the night sky.

"I'm sorry," she mumbled.

He said nothing.

She turned toward him and repeated, "I'm sorry."

"I heard you the first time."

"Oh." She slumped down to the floor. "I told you this wasn't a good idea. I'll find another place to live tomorrow."

He didn't enjoy seeing her like this. He preferred the feisty, outspoken woman he had met in New York. "That's the answer. Run away again."

"I didn't run away. I went for a walk."

"To Boston? Paul Revere covered less ground on his midnight ride."

"Don't be sarcastic."

"Why? Is that right reserved only for you?"

"I said I was sorry. What do you want from me?"

He wanted trust. Was that more than she could give? "You know, I've given up expecting anything from the Hawthorne family. I thought it would take a little longer for you to become one of them."

Her eyes narrowed. "That's not fair."

"Neither is you believing anything that William and Joseph would say." He tossed the folder on the bed.

"What's that?"

"The papers you wanted to see. About the kidnapping and the information from the private investigator. By the way, they located your stepfather. He's not involved. The report is on the top."

"Oh."

He paused at the door and turned back. "For the record, who you are doesn't make a damn bit of difference to me."

"You might not say that if you knew the whole truth about me."

He shook his head. "I thought you knew me better than that."

Clayton left and the room felt as empty as her heart. She walked over to the bed and picked up the folder. The thick file clearly would contain a thorough account of the kidnapping as well as a detailed investigation of her. She thought about Clayton. The contents didn't seem as important now as they had yesterday.

An heiress? Her? She was an *airhead.* Her stomach rumbled but not from hunger. Had she screwed up the only good thing in her life? Her juvenile probation officer had warned her that her defensive attitude would land her in trouble someday. Defiance had been her shield, sarcasm her sword as she tried to survive a life she'd found loathsome.

She dropped the folder on the bed. The past could wait. The present couldn't. She stepped into the hall. Silence mocked her. Had he retired so early?

She hesitated at the door. In the ten days she had been living in the condo she had never entered Clayton's bedroom. Because she'd had so little control over her life as a child, she had insisted on complete control as an adult. To enter meant to surrender the part of herself she had thus far held back. Everything had been on her terms.

Her reign of power was over. She couldn't fight, joke or seduce her way out of this one.

He had conveniently left the door ajar. There was a time when his cocksure attitude would have caused her to retreat to a neutral corner and wait him out. She had neither the willpower nor the patience for a sexual standoff.

"Clayton?" She stepped inside. A sliver of light from the hall illuminated his back and shoulder. "Are you asleep?"

He didn't answer.

"I know you're awake. It's only nine o'clock."

"Then why did you ask if I was sleeping?"

She inched closer to the king-size bed and sat on the edge. "Did you know that your bed is in two different time zones?"

"What do you want?" He wasn't going to make this easy for her.

"Would you look at me?"

Flipping over, he propped himself on one elbow. The sheet fell to his waist, revealing the rippling muscles of his chest. His hair was rumpled and falling across his forehead.

"I'm sorry I didn't trust you," she said. "It won't happen again."

He stared at her for a long moment, his steady gaze giving away none of his emotions. "Take off your shirt."

"What?" His surprising command caught her off guard.

"Take it off."

Her heart thumped against her ribs. Did he mean to

humiliate her to get even? She hadn't figured him for a vengeful person, but she had never seen him hurt before. Although her mind protested, she blindly followed his order.

"The bra, too."

"Why?"

"Because I want you to."

Her trembling fingers fumbled helplessly with the back clasp. She tried to keep in mind Alicia's assurance that Clayton would never hurt her. He obviously had a point to make, and she owed him the right to make it.

"What now?" she asked, while fighting the urge to cover herself.

"The rest."

Taking a deep, calming breath, she removed her shorts and panties at the same time. The cool air-conditioning sent a chill through her. She wrapped her arms around her bent knees.

"No. Lie down on the bed," he said quietly.

She searched his face for a trace of humor or tenderness, but his expression was blank. Her courage was fading. Before she lost all her nerve, she uncurled her body and stretched out next to him.

He slid his hand across her stomach and pulled her closer. His warm breath caressed her ear. The closeness had all the makings of erotic foreplay, but she instinctively knew that wasn't what Clayton had in mind.

"Next Saturday is the Westlake Charity Ball. I want you to go as my date."

Her jaw dropped open. For several surreal seconds she couldn't compose a logical thought. Finally she muttered, "You made me strip to ask me on a date."

"I didn't *make* you do anything, Mikki."

"Don't argue semantics."

"There's a big difference. You always had the option to refuse."

"And you would have been mad at me for the rest of your natural life."

"I never gave you an ultimatum. Any threat you felt was purely in your imagination."

"Like earlier," she said, making the connection. "You wanted to see if I trust you now?"

He cupped his hand over her chin. "I wanted *you* to see if you trusted me enough to let down your guard and be utterly defenseless."

Slowly her smile returned. "You know how to make me lose control."

"I didn't want you to lose it. I wanted you to give it up."

She snuggled against him. "And now that I have?"

"We talk about the charity ball. It's boring, pretentious and filled with snobs who make your cousins seem humble."

"Sounds charming."

"It gets better. You need one of those dresses that costs more than you make in a week, so I'm paying for it."

Her first impulse was to decline the offer of a dress or the ball. The thought of being indebted to anyone galled her. But Clayton wasn't *anyone*.

He grinned mischievously. "One dress won't make you a kept woman. And I promise you won't have to put out at the end of the night."

As her words came back to haunt her, a warm flush crept up her cheeks. "Why do you want to go with me?"

"I wouldn't want my friends to think I couldn't get a date."

She stroked her fingers over his chest. "I don't think that would be a problem for you."

"Would you prefer I ask another woman?"

"I'd hate it," she admitted fiercely, stunned by her sudden surge of possessiveness. "Okay, I'll go. But if I have to play Cinderella at some pretentious ball, I will definitely expect you to put out at the end of the evening."

His throaty chuckle echoed in her ear. "That's a lot of pressure. I suppose you would expect to be satisfied. No quickie in the back of the limo?"

She swallowed a laugh. He was beginning to sound like her. "You betcha."

"I can live with that, but it could require hours of practice between now and then."

The last of her nervousness drained away. Their argument—or whatever it had been—was over now. She closed her hand around his full arousal and sighed longingly. "I'm willing to do my part."

"Mine, too, if I don't stop you." He put his hands on her shoulders and pushed her firmly onto her back. Catching her wrists in his large hands, he pinned her arms above her head.

"I'm a bit of a control freak, huh?"

He lowered himself on top of her. "You made progress today."

"Okay. You run the show tonight."

He released her arms only to bury his fingers in her hair. "If that's a challenge, I'm up for it."

Eyes closed, she wriggled beneath him. "I can tell." Her body tensed in anticipation. As always, the feel of him made her impatient for more.

With practiced ease, he stroked his hands over the contours of her waist and hip, savoring each curve as if he wanted to commit them to memory. His unhurried exploration gave rise to an overwhelming urgency inside of her. She wanted him now, but they were playing by his rules and he preferred a slow, exquisite exercise in frustration.

He rubbed his knee along her inner thigh. A hot coil in her abdomen unraveled to a ribbon of heat spreading through her. He sprinkled a line of kisses along her shoulder to the base of her throat. His tongue drew circles of moist warmth over her stomach, traveling lower with each tender stroke.

"You still with me?"

She opened her eyes and stared at him desperately. "Don't stop now." Her words came out in a pleading moan.

He sucked in a deep breath. With just a look or a single whispered word she touched a place inside him he hadn't known existed. Nothing mattered but her.

As if he had been hit in the head with a lead pipe, realization shocked him into immobility. This odd feeling he hadn't been able to identify must be love.

"What's wrong?" Her eyes narrowed in concern.

He shook his head. "Everything's perfect."

In truth, everything about her was perfect. However, he didn't trust perfection in correlation to his life. He had given up on the possibility of long-term happiness. But as he gazed into Mikki's eyes, he could almost believe.

"If you're trying to drive me crazy, you've succeeded," she muttered breathlessly. Although she had relegated control to him, he might not keep it if he held back any longer.

His fingers probed the downy softness between her legs. He found the sensitive bud at the center and stroked the tip until she writhed beneath his touch and cried out his name. Then, he did it again.

"You want me?" he asked, although he knew the answer.

"Desperately." She opened for him.

He entered her easily. She arched upward to meet him, welcome him. By silent mutual consent they established a rhythm that began fast and escalated to frenzied. Her desire rivaled his own and she matched his every movement.

As he thrust deep inside her, she clung to him. Her soft sexy groans and involuntary sighs of excitement gave life to the silent night.

She convulsed around him, triggering his own wild, surging climax. An explosion so powerful that he felt something shatter. Could that something be the wall he had built around his heart?

They lay entwined for a long time afterward. He never tired of staring at her. Once he'd glimpsed perfection, it was hard to look away. Humming softly and smiling, she looked as content as a kitten after a saucer of milk. Languorously, she stretched her arms above her head and sighed.

"Tired?" he asked.

"Worn out. May I sleep here tonight?"

What an odd question, he thought. "I assumed you would."

"I never assume, and then I'm rarely disappointed."

It felt right to have her in his bed, in his life. Did she still have doubts? If so, were those doubts about him, or herself? He knew he should ask, but he wasn't sure he wanted to know the answer.

Twelve

Mikki stared at the clear blue water. When Richard had invited her to spend the day at his house, she had thought she was ready. An afternoon sunning by the pool was safe enough. From the moment she had stepped through the gate, though, a knot formed in the pit of her stomach. After two hours she still avoided the edge of the pool.

Rather than admit to her irrational fears, she told Richard she wanted to work on her tan for the Charity Ball that evening. They ate lunch on the deck, then she was left to deal with her anxiety again. Normally she loved water. She remembered Richard's account of Meg's fall in the pool. If she was reliving suppressed memories, why had she never had this reaction before?

She was no closer to understanding her fears when Clayton joined her. Looking incredibly sexy in his royal blue bathing trunks, he strolled toward her with athletic grace. His presence cleared her mind of unpleasant thoughts. She rose from the lounge chair to meet him.

"I thought you went for a haircut," she said, running her fingers through the silky chestnut locks.

"I did."

"How can you tell? It looks the same as this morning."

"That's the idea."

"Oh, I see. Every two weeks on schedule, right?"

His lips curved into a frown of mild annoyance. "Are you going to pick on me today?"

"It's not my first choice of what I'd like to do with you, but..." She brushed against him and sighed.

"I think you need to cool off." He caught her around the waist and walked toward the edge.

Her reaction was swift and violent. A shriek nearly split his eardrum. She grabbed his shoulders with such force, her fingernails broke skin. As she twisted and turned to free herself, he fought to keep from dropping her.

"Okay, okay." He took a step back and lowered her to the deck. "Calm down."

She shook uncontrollably. Her eyes, wide and round with terror, glared accusingly. A strange response from a woman who could spend hours in the water.

"What happened?"

"I don't know," she managed to get out between deep gulps of air.

He pulled her into his arms and stroked her back until she stopped trembling. In his peripheral vision he saw Joseph approach, followed closely by his brother. Clayton groaned. The last thing she needed was grief from her cousins.

"Are you all right, Meg?" Joseph's concern sounded genuine despite the slurred words.

"Yes." Her voice faltered. She stepped out of Clayton's arms and reached for her T-shirt.

Joseph nodded. "Bad memories have a way of coming back to haunt us."

Mikki raised her head and stared intently.

Clayton let out a grunt. "Memories of an accidental tumble in the pool when she was three? I doubt that."

"What if it wasn't an accident?" Joseph asked. "What if that tumble had been a deliberate throw?"

William clamped a hand on his brother's shoulder. "Shut up. You're drunk."

"Not that drunk. I know what I saw."

"Keep your delusional fantasies to yourself. You didn't see anything." William's voice rang with warning.

Clayton folded his arms across his chest. "I'd like to hear more."

Had the Hawthorne brothers kept certain facts from Richard all these years? He gazed at Mikki, who seemed fascinated and repulsed at the same time.

"Why not ask Alicia?" Joseph asked. "She saw the whole thing, too."

"She would have said something," Clayton said with certainty. His aunt would not have allowed anyone to harm Meg.

"She tried. No one took her seriously. They thought she was hysterical. After all, Father was family, she wasn't." Joseph shrugged what appeared to be an apology. "You know how that goes, don't you, Clay?"

William muttered several expletives. "He doesn't know what he's saying."

The younger Hawthorne drew up his frame. "I'm

getting damn tired of you telling me that. Father despised Uncle Richard for his success the way you despise Clayton. And if you think I'm lying, just take a look at Meg's expression.'' Joseph turned toward her. "You remember, don't you?"

Mikki's face reflected her confusion and fear. "I'm not sure."

"I wouldn't be surprised to find out dear old Dad was the one who had you snatched." Apparently Joseph had held his feelings for a long time. He looked relieved by his admission, however late it had come.

William kicked a lounge chair. "This is all a bunch of bull. The truth is, she was with Alicia and Clay when it happened. If anyone's to blame, they are."

"Stop it!" Her piercing scream caught the attention of all three men. "It doesn't matter who or why."

"You never should have returned from the dead." William glowered at her, then stormed away. Joseph looked as if he wanted to say more, but he, too, went back to the house.

Mikki tried to absorb all she had heard. Now she knew who had made the threatening calls. The rush of adrenaline had slowed, but her heart still pounded with apprehension. "How much of Joseph's rambling was truth?"

Clayton laced his fingers through hers and led her to the lounge chair. "It's hard to tell."

"Was Richard's brother capable of such evil?"

"Capable? He was bitter about Richard's success, but that's taking sibling rivalry to the extreme."

Mikki sat in the chair next to Clayton. There was a sorrow in his expression that touched her heart. "Were you really there when Meg was kidnapped?"

"It's in the reports I gave you."

"I haven't read them yet." In the past week she hadn't given the file more than a curious glance. Had she been avoiding the truth? "So were you?"

"Yes."

"And they've made your life hell since?"

"Not mine. Alicia's."

"Richard, too?"

Clayton shook his head. "No. He stood by her. But then, he stood by his brother, too. That's his nature."

"How strange." Richard had reason to distrust the world, yet he naively trusted everyone, including her. The more she learned, the less she understood.

Draping an arm across her shoulder, Clayton urged her closer. "If you want to forget about tonight..."

"I'm fine. Or I will be. Right now, I'm going to get myself into that pool. I can't live the rest of my life being afraid of ghosts."

Mikki tugged at the bodice of her strapless evening gown. She was half afraid the top would fall off, although Alicia had assured her it wouldn't. If she managed not to trip on the bottom of the dress, the night would be a success.

While she appreciated the offer of preparing for the charity ball at Richard's house, she would have gladly traded the help of the live-in staff for ten minutes alone with Clayton. Her nerves were as tight as the knot in her stomach. *Please don't let me embarrass myself,* she silently prayed.

Richard had asked her to meet him in the study. She could only guess what he wanted to talk about. Her heels clacked against the tiles as she crossed the foyer, echoing a hollow beat. Taking a deep breath for courage, she rapped her knuckles on the door.

"Come in." Richard's cheerful voice welcomed her. He rose to greet her with a smile as warm as the sun. "You look gorgeous."

"Gorgeous? This dress is obscene."

"Why, it's perfectly respectable."

She let out a nervous laugh. "I meant the price. There can't be more than four yards of material, and that was imported from a country with no child labor laws. Not to mention that it was manufactured in a nonunion shop."

He chuckled heartily. "Oh, well, I hope I don't further offend your sense of propriety when I give you this."

She glanced at the velvet box in his hand, then returned her gaze to him. "What is it?"

"For you, Mikki. Open it."

That he had called her Mikki rather than Meg wasn't lost on her. She lifted the top and viewed a magnificent diamond choker and matching ear clips.

"It's—" She searched for the right word to describe the beautiful piece. "—spectacular."

"A family heirloom."

"I can't accept it. You should give this to Alicia."

He shook his head. "I think that would be in poor taste."

"Why? She is your wife."

"Yes, but these pieces came from your mother's family."

A hard lump formed in her throat, threatening to choke her. Her eyes brimmed with salty tears, and she prayed she wouldn't cry. How unfair she had been to Richard all this time! Wouldn't any parent feel a burning need to know what had happened to his only child? She was safe from her stepfather's reach. She no longer felt the need to protect her mother. Even Richard's nephews were no real threat. The only obstacle left to overcome was her own fear of the truth.

"Why don't we wait until—" Her voice broke and she sucked in a large gulp of air.

"They're yours to keep no matter what happens. I have no use for them."

She had gotten what she had wanted. Acceptance on her terms. Why did she feel this stifling pain in her chest? Was it because she believed, as certainly as Richard, that he was her father? "I don't know what to say."

"Don't say anything. You go have a good time tonight and maybe tomorrow we'll talk again."

She nodded. For the first time in her life, words failed her.

Mikki smiled for what seemed like the millionth time. Clayton had not exaggerated. The event was boring, pretentious, and contained the largest congregation of snobs east of Beverly Hills. Absently she fingered the necklace. She had not been able to forget the look of paternal admiration on Richard's face when she had put the piece on.

"You seem lost," Clayton whispered in her ear. Since he had deserted her to discuss business earlier, she had felt a bit lost.

"When are you going to dance with me?" she asked.

"Dance?" he repeated as if the idea were inconceivable.

"Yes, dance. You hold me close, we move to the music. The concept is simple." She laced her fingers through his and pulled him toward the dance floor. The need to be in his arms was more than she could fight.

"Do you promise not to lead?"

"I'll try." She laid one hand on his shoulder and the other right across his rear end.

"Mikki," he groaned.

Her eyes widened innocently. "Sorry. I misjudged. You're taller than I thought."

"Can't you behave?" He laughed. "Never mind. I forgot who I was talking to."

They swayed together in a slow, sensual rhythm. She drank in the musky smell of him, a scent more intoxicating than the imported champagne being served. Resting her cheek against the satin lapel of his tuxedo, she closed her eyes and sighed.

"You've been very quiet tonight."

"I thought it best to keep my foot out of my mouth. I'd choke on my heels."

He pressed a kiss against her forehead. "No jokes. What's on your mind?"

As an opening, she wouldn't get a better one. "I think it's time to take that blood test."

He tensed slightly. "Are you sure?"

"I'm not sure of anything anymore. I think it's time to get some answers." While she had her courage, she continued, "But before I do, there are some things about me that I have to tell you."

"Do you want to leave?"

"After the dance." She needed to feel his arms around her for a while longer. Her life was about to change once again, but this time she would have no control over the outcome.

Mikki walked through the front door and kicked off her shoes. Despite Clayton's best efforts to draw her out, she had been silent during the ride home. He had prepared himself for the worst. No matter what she told him, he would not react. What she had done was in the past.

"Would you like a drink?" he asked.

She shook her head. Her eyes shimmered with moisture and her bottom lip quivered. Taking his hands, she led him into the living room.

He noted the faint scent of sandalwood as she pressed her body close to him. She stroked her fingers over his hands, his arms and chest. The purely sensual feeling sent shock waves through him. Her lips brushed his, but as he reached for her, she took a step back.

"Sit down for a minute," she said softly.

"All right." He lowered himself onto the sofa.

"Hold out your hands."

He shrugged and cupped his hands together. She dropped a handful of jewelry into his open palms. His cufflinks, tie clip, ring and watch.

"Very good," he said drily.

"I don't think you understand."

"Sure I do. You're a talented pickpocket. I knew that after the first time I met you. But you've returned everything."

"I didn't used to. And I wasn't always talented. I have a long arrest record that began when I was thirteen."

Less than a year after her "mother" had married Maxwell Blake, he'd begun to use Mikki in his scams. That didn't surprise Clayton. "And?"

"You want details?"

"Only if you wish to give them. I'm aware of your

adoptive family background. I'm sure you didn't have a choice."

She flopped down next to him on the sofa. Her legs tangled in the flowing skirt of her dress, and she yanked the fabric up to her knees with a frustrated hiss. "It's too easy to blame Max. Truth is, I knew what I was doing. I could have turned him in to the police."

"Why didn't you?"

"My mom. Max had a violent temper. As long as I did as I was told, he left us alone. In a way, that was my power over him. If he had struck either one of us, I would have turned him in."

He slipped an arm across her shoulders. "So that only proves you're loyal to those you love."

"And foolish in my choices. She wasn't my real mother. I could have dealt with that, but she never told me. Max did, the day she died. I left right after the funeral and never looked back."

He smiled ruefully. "Until I came into your life and forced you to?"

"Not really. I'm not proud of that time in my life, so it's never been far from my mind no matter how hard I try to forget."

"As far as I can tell, you have nothing to be ashamed of. If your 'mother' had gone to the same lengths to protect you as you went to protect her, it never would have happened."

A lone tear streamed down her cheek. "She wasn't my mother."

"You didn't know that. And unless you decide to write your memoirs, no one else will know about your past. It's what you do with the rest of your life that matters."

"You don't care?" She wiped the back of her hand across her face.

"No. It doesn't change the way I feel about you."

"And how is that?" she asked.

His heart skipped a beat. There was nothing more constricting than being put on the spot. "Excuse me?"

"How do you feel about me?"

He loosened the tie at his neck. "What do you think?"

"I think you just sidestepped the question."

For a long moment he couldn't formulate a reply. He knew what he felt for her. Why couldn't he tell her?

"Never mind. It wasn't a fair question," she said.

"I didn't think you needed to hear the words."

"I'd like to hear them once in my life."

"I don't suppose you'd let me say it with a Hallmark card?" he suggested hopefully.

"No!"

"You know, you've never told me how you feel about me, either."

Mikki exhaled an exasperated sigh. "I let you take over my life. I put on this ridiculous dress for you. I wash your underwear, for heaven's sake. If that's not love, I don't know what is."

He laughed. "I think it's debatable who took over whose life. I plan to take that ridiculous dress off for you and I have granted you the honor of washing my underwear. So our love must be mutual."

She stared at him for several silent seconds. "Aren't we a pathetic couple of cowards? We can't even express our feelings without making a joke of them."

He held her face in his hands. "I love you. No matter what you did or who you are."

"Me, too."

"Mikki!"

"Okay, okay. I love you." Her softly spoken words reflected a pain he failed to understand.

"Then why do you look like you lost your best friend rather than found him?"

"Because the people I love always end up leaving me."

He kissed her trembling mouth. "I'm not going anywhere."

"Not right now, maybe."

"Not ever."

"It's not a promise you can make." She locked her arms around his neck and held him so tightly, she shook.

His heart broke for the young girl who'd had her childhood stolen from her. For the teenager who'd been forced to grow up too early. And mostly for the woman who didn't believe she deserved a chance at happiness.

Thirteen

Mikki paced the floor of the study. After the longest four days of her life, the results of the blood test were due today. Figuring that she would be useless at work, Clayton suggested she take the day off and wait with Richard for the call from the lab. The idea sounded good until she realized that the results might be negative. With Richard sitting five feet away, smiling indulgently, she wasn't sure how she would handle bad news.

"It's early, Mikki. Sit down."

She plopped down in the leather chair and twisted her fingers together in her lap. "What time is it?"

"Three minutes later than the last time you asked me. I don't know what you're worried about. The doctor already said that the odds are on your side."

"I'm not a gambler."

"You've read the reports. Two days after the kidnapping, Sara Finnley moved with her daughter Michelle to McAfee, Kansas, yet no one seems to remember her having a child before then.''

''Coincidence.'' Mikki didn't believe that any more than Richard. Too many facts about her mother's life didn't add up. Granted, the investigator had to rely on the twenty-year-old memories of college roommates and friends. By all accounts Sara had come into money in her senior year of college and had dropped out to claim a house in Kansas.

Why hadn't she finished school and then claimed the house? How did she come to have a child when she had never mentioned one to her closest friends? Something in the reports struck a chord, but Mikki couldn't say what. She felt as if the past was a jigsaw puzzle with the center piece missing. The one piece that tied the whole picture together.

''Mikki?''

She glanced at Richard. ''Sorry. I'm distracted.'' She shook her head. If there was something to find, Clayton and Richard would have found it by now. They had gone over the papers for five months and come up with nothing.

Her mind kept returning to Sara as a high school girl. The daughter of a working-class, Irish father and a Navajo mother, she had attended a prestigious prep school in Tempe, Arizona, on an academic scholarship. Why had a woman who had shown such promise become involved in a kidnapping four years later? How had she come into money when no ransom had been exchanged?

The shrill ring of the telephone brought Mikki to her feet with a start. Richard snapped up the receiver before the second ring. She tried to read his poker face. He gave nothing away as he listened to the person at the other end.

"Thank you," he said, and placed the phone back in the cradle. "Well, Mikki."

Mikki, not Meg. Her heart sank.

"Or may I now call you Megan again?" he added, and grinned from ear to ear.

A shudder ran through her and her body broke out in a cold sweat. "That was mean."

"So you *do* care," he noted with obvious relief.

She pushed her hair from her face and exhaled slowly. "Of course I do."

"Then why act like you didn't?"

"Because I didn't want to hope."

His eyes held love. "Hope was all I had to hold on to. But now that the lab has confirmed what I already knew, we have things to take care of. We'll have to tell the family. Then the police will have to be informed. The case was never officially closed."

"I have to call Clayton." She wanted to share the news with him.

"Yes. Tell him to bring your things when he comes."

"What do you mean?"

"You'll be moving home, of course."

Sorrow ripped at her heart. "Oh, Richard. If I led you to believe that, I'm sorry. I told you I didn't expect anything from you."

"You're my daughter."

She knelt down beside him and covered his hand with hers. "I'm twenty-three years old. I'm not the little girl you lost."

His dark eyes shimmered with moisture. "Are you saying it's too late for us?"

"It's too late to get back the past. That doesn't mean we can't go forward. But you'll have to accept that I'm an adult and I have to live my life my way." Not that working in her father's company and living with the boss was flaunting her independence.

After a long hesitation, he nodded a weary agreement. "Okay, Meg. But if things don't work out, you can come here."

"You don't think they will?"

"I don't know. Just a few weeks ago you were complaining about how he infuriated you."

She laughed. Clayton had an uncanny ability for getting her hot under the collar—and a few other places, too. "That hasn't changed."

"Are you in love with him?"

She nodded. "Does that bother you?"

"Clayton's like a son to me, but to tell you the truth, I never thought of him as a son-in-law."

Son-in-law? Marriage? The subject had never come up between them. While Clayton wanted the blood test to be positive for Richard's and Alicia's sakes, she got the impression that he would prefer that she was Michelle Finnley, an unknown orphan from Kansas.

Would this new twist affect their relationship? The possibility had always been there, but she hadn't prepared herself for the reality.

"Are you staying for dinner?" Richard asked.

Hearing the echo of hope in his voice, she couldn't refuse. Her talk with Clayton would have to wait.

Clayton left the office immediately after Mikki's call. Although she claimed to be all right, he heard the unspoken plea in her voice. Despite his constant assurances that the outcome made no difference to him, she still seemed to doubt his feelings.

It took nearly an hour to battle the city traffic. By the time he arrived at the estate, she had gone out. He met his aunt in the salon. She looked serene and peaceful for the first time in a long time.

"I guess you heard the good news," she said.

He nodded. "Where's Mikki?"

"With Richard. He took her to the bank to get her birth certificate from the safe-deposit box. They'll be back for dinner. Why don't you go take a rest until then."

"I need to talk to you about something."

She smiled. "What's on your mind, dear?"

He loosened his tie and sat on the sofa across from her. "Joseph said something last week that bothered me. What happened that day when Richard's brother pulled Meg out of the pool?"

Her complexion paled and she shifted nervously. "Why bring that up now? It was twenty years ago."

"I want to know."

"What did Joseph say?"

"I think you know."

She fidgeted with her necklace. "You know how Joseph gets when he drinks."

His aunt had never been evasive with him. "Did David deliberately try to harm her?"

"What difference could it possibly make now? He's dead."

"It might explain what happened afterward. Don't you think it's ironic that those papers were sent to Richard within a week of David's death?"

"And?"

"I think he was involved in her kidnapping."

"I wouldn't run that past Richard if I were you. You know he won't listen to anything about his brother."

"Is that why you never told Richard?"

Her face darkened with anger. "I told him. He didn't believe me. Maybe if Joseph had spoken up sooner..." She sucked in a large gulp of air. "I tried to warn Richard that Meg was in danger. They all thought I was in shock and incapable of distinguishing the facts. I never mentioned the incident again."

"Even after the abduction?"

"What good would it have done? To blame someone else only casts suspicion on yourself. I didn't need help there, did I? The nanny marries the millionaire, and the child suddenly disappears. It's a classic movie-of-the-week plot."

"Richard never blamed you."

"He never accused me. The blame has always been mine."

His insides twisted with the same helpless rage he had carried since childhood. "You couldn't have prevented it any more than I could."

She smiled sadly. "And yet you, too, blamed yourself for years, didn't you?"

He stared out the window. His aunt was right on all counts. Perhaps he should let the matter rest for the family's sake as well as his own. What good would the truth do now? Richard had his daughter back. Was there a point to destroying the memory of a man who was dead? He saw firsthand what that had done to Mikki.

His aunt rose and stifled a yawn. "I think I'll take a short nap before dinner. It's been a hectic day." Her features were etched in sorrow, and he felt guilty for reminding her of painful memories.

"I'm sorry if I upset you."

"You could never do that." She patted his shoulder on the way out.

Clayton tried to get his mind off the events of the past. Where he went from here was all that mattered. He reached for the *New York Times*. Before he could find the financial section, Mikki walked into the salon, her dark ponytail bobbing to the spring in her step. The sun reflected off her rhinestone sunglasses and sent prisms of light darting around the room. He couldn't read her eyes behind the dark lenses.

"You're slipping, Clayton. Your tie is loose before five o'clock. What's next? Pastel-colored shirts and plaid sports jackets?"

"Never." If she felt up to picking on his wardrobe, she must be all right. "Where's your father?"

"I think he needed his heart medicine. He let me drive home."

"What? You don't have a license."

She pushed the glasses up on her head and glared down at him. "So what's your point?"

"You get caught and you won't be able to get one."

"Then it's a good thing I didn't stop when I side-swiped that car."

"You didn't!"

"No, I didn't. But thanks for the vote of confidence. You don't grow up in Kansas without learning how to drive a truck before you're twelve."

He shook his head. "I can't believe Richard let you drive."

"Did *you* ever try to say no to her?" Richard asked as he entered the room.

Mikki laughed and dropped down onto the sofa,

landing half in Clayton's lap. "He tells me no all the time, but it doesn't get him anywhere."

"I rest my case, Clay."

She smiled impishly.

Clayton could only pray that she retained her free-spirited exuberance when the rest of the family heard the news at dinner. "So tell me. What do you want me to call you now?"

"Call me yours." She pursed her lips together and batted her eyelashes. Over the weeks he had learned to read her moods. Joking helped her to avoid subjects she didn't want to deal with.

"Where's Alicia?" Richard asked.

Clayton grasped Mikki's wrist as she tugged at his tie. He shot her a warning glare that had no effect, then gave up and returned his attention to Richard. "She's in her room, resting."

"I think I'll join her."

"See, you've embarrassed your father," he muttered.

Richard laughed and called over his shoulder, "I beg to differ, Clay. I'm not the one with the red face."

Once they were alone, he pinned her arms behind her and let out a low groan. "You are obnoxious."

"I've missed you."

"Don't try to distract me."

"I want you," she whispered in his ear.

"Right words, wrong place."

She wrinkled her nose. "One little kiss."

"You don't know the meaning of one little kiss, and I forget it once you start."

"One kiss—no tongue, no hands. Is it a deal?"

He nodded reluctantly and let her go. A tactical error, he discovered. She had no intention of keeping her word, and he didn't have the desire to hold her to it.

There was more than passion in her kiss. It was as if she needed to know that he still wanted her. She tested him to the limit, then slowly, almost apologetically, she drew back.

"Mikki," she whispered.

"What?"

"I still want you to call me Mikki."

He held her snugly in his embrace. "I don't think I could call you anything else."

Mikki picked at the salmon mousse without enthusiasm. She had lost her appetite before the soup had been served. Since Richard's announcement, pleasant conversation had ceased.

Joseph, looking somber and surprisingly sober, clamped his hand over his brother's shoulder as William tried to leave the table. Tension, as thick as morning fog, blanketed the room. Another happy dinner with the Hawthorne family, Mikki thought.

All the peace and happiness that had surrounded Richard this afternoon seemed to dissolve in a sea of disappointment. Surely he didn't think that a piece of paper from a lab would guarantee her an instant welcome. Was her father naive or merely out of touch with the reality of his family?

Alicia covered her husband's hand and smiled affectionately toward Mikki. "So, Meg, what are your plans now?"

She squirmed in her seat. "The same as they were yesterday. I've been checking into taking some classes at Boston U in the fall."

William snickered. "Sure, now that Uncle Richard will foot the bills."

"Like he did for us?" Joseph sniped, to the visible surprise of the others. "Why don't you back off? She's your cousin."

"When did you become her biggest fan?" William asked. "Last I heard you thought she was a gold-digging, street hust—"

Richard brought his fist down on the table, like a judge banging a gavel. "I will not tolerate this rude behavior. Apologize to Meg immediately."

Mikki shook her head. "I don't want an apology. I don't want anything at all from him." She gazed at her father's face, scarlet with rage. "You can't force people to feel things they don't. If that upsets you, then maybe we should meet somewhere else."

"My daughter should not be made to feel like an outsider in my home."

"And they shouldn't, either. It's their home, too, but it's not mine. And I am more than capable of standing up for myself when I've had enough. Isn't that right, Clayton?"

Clayton raised his glass in a salute and smiled. How was he able to ignore the animosity going on around him? Would she ever reach a point where she could overlook the suspicion and distrust?

"While Meg is being more than generous, I will not put up with this kind of behavior again. Have I made myself clear?" Richard asked pointedly.

William glowered at his uncle. "If she's Megan, then what happened? Why wasn't she found sooner?"

"I don't know yet, but I will. If I have to trace every person that ever knew Sara Finnley since the day she

was born, I will find out how Meg came to be adopted
by that woman.''

Mikki glanced around the table. No one seemed
pleased by Richard's pronouncement. No one! Her
cousins' cold reception came as no surprise. They were
afraid the trail would lead to their father. Clayton, who
understood the mixed emotions she felt for the woman
she knew as her mother, lowered his head sadly.

Alicia slipped her turquoise and silver necklace
down the front of her dress. The gesture was innocent
enough. Why did Mikki feel the start of a double knot
forming in her stomach? She closed her eyes and pic-
tured the intricate Navajo piece Alicia felt the need to
hide.

A chill ran down her spine. Now she knew what it
was about Sara Finnley's background that struck a
chord in her. And she was fairly certain she knew what
had happened to her. What she couldn't figure out was
Why?

Fourteen

Excuses to leave flew across the table faster than an SST. While Richard cornered Clayton in the study, Mikki decided to follow Alicia to her sitting room. She watched from the doorway as the older woman nervously straightened articles that weren't out of place.

Suddenly Alicia turned and let out a startled cry. Her hand flew to her mouth. "Meg. You frightened me. I thought you were with Richard."

Mikki shrugged. "He's busy with Clayton."

"Business, no doubt. You get used to it." Alicia pointed to a chair. "Have a seat."

Mikki lowered herself into the chair and waited for Alicia to do the same. "They're discussing the kidnapping."

"That's only natural. Ever since that envelope arrived, Richard has talked of nothing else. Even that scare with his heart didn't slow him down."

"He's determined to find out what happened," Mikki said.

"I guess you are, too."

"I thought I was." If this was where the truth was leading, she wasn't sure anymore.

"And now?"

"I'd like to know why."

Alicia tipped her head. "I suppose that's natural, too."

"I was hoping you would tell me."

The color drained from Alicia's face. "Me?"

"Your necklace. The one you had on at dinner. It's Navajo, I believe."

"Yes."

"Did you get it in Arizona? You used to live there, didn't you?"

"Yes. I still have some friends there."

"Was Sara Finnley one of them? She grew up there, too," Mikki said. "But you knew that, didn't you? Was she a friend?"

"No. She wasn't a friend," Alicia said softly.

"But you knew her?"

She wouldn't meet Mikki's eyes as she answered, "Yes. Sara was a cousin of Clayton's father."

"Why did you do it?"

"I don't think you would understand."

"Did you hate me that much?" Even as she spoke the words, her heart rejected the notion. Alicia's affection was genuine. Of that, Mikki was sure.

"No. No, Meg. I loved you like my own, but I couldn't keep you safe."

"From what?" She thought about her jinx. *You were the most accident-prone child.* Joseph's revelation, *What if that accidental tumble had been a deliberate throw?* Even her strange reaction to the pool made sense now. "What Joseph said about Richard's brother was true."

"Yes. I believe he intended to kill you, and I just didn't feel I had a choice. So I arranged your abduction with Sara and her brothers. I was able to keep tabs on you through friends until Sara married Max. She cut off contact with her family after you all moved."

"How did you find me?"

"I didn't. Clayton did."

"He knew?" she exclaimed.

"No!" Alicia grabbed Mikki's hand. "I sent the envelope anonymously. I knew Richard would insist Clayton track you down."

"Why? You had to know there was a chance they would trace it back to you."

"I don't care. David is dead. He can't hurt you anymore." Alicia's voice broke. She grabbed the arms of the seat to stop the trembling in her hands. Her composure regained, she raised her chin. "If you don't mind, I'd like to be the one who tells Richard. I'm ready to pay for what I did."

Mikki thought about her father. What would this kind of news do to him? Half the truth would destroy him, and the entire truth might kill him. And what would a full disclosure do to the rest of the family? Wasn't it enough that Mikki knew what had happened and why?

"Unfortunately you aren't the only one who will pay. Are you willing to hurt William and Joseph by publicly coming forward about David Hawthorne? Because if you aren't, I see no point in coming forward with your part in the whole affair."

"I've lived with this secret too long already."

"And you'll continue to live with it. If you feel you have to pay, then that will be your punishment. I will not allow you to do that to Richard, or Clayton. Have you thought about what that would do to them?"

"Every day of my life." Alicia expelled a deep breath and sighed. "I think I'd better tell Clay."

"A little late for confessions."

Mikki gasped at the sound of Clayton's embittered voice. She turned and locked her gaze on him. His gray eyes looked as cold as steel. No need to ask how much he'd overheard. His expression said it all.

"Let me explain," Alicia said in a whispered plea.

"I heard your explanation. I don't care to hear anything more from you." Behind his barely contained fury echoed a pain so deep that Mikki winced.

She went to him to offer comfort, but he wouldn't accept it. He recoiled from her touch, erecting an invisible and unbreakable wall.

"I'm leaving," he said.

"I'll get my things."

"No! You belong here with your father, where you should have been all along." He spun on his heel and walked out without so much as a glimpse in his aunt's direction.

Mikki glanced at Alicia's dejected frame slumped over in the chair. *Sometimes we do the wrong thing for the right reason.* Is this what the older woman had meant?

She ran after Clayton, grabbing his sleeve in a vise-like grip to stop him. "At least talk to your aunt before you go storming off."

"I have nothing to say to her."

"And me? You have nothing to say to me?"

He pried her fingers loose. For a second she thought

she saw a spark of hope in his eyes, but just as quickly it vanished. "You're better off here."

Did he honestly believe that? "I don't agree."

"You will eventually."

"Can we talk about this?"

He stared blankly. What was going on in his mind? From their first meeting in New York, he had exhibited a wide range of emotions, but never had she seen such a lack of feeling. It was as if something had died inside him. He strode away, disappearing down the staircase.

Clayton had promised to stand by her no matter what happened. As long as someone in her family was to blame, he should have added. The feelings of betrayal she could understand, but what would he accomplish by pushing her away, too?

A tightness squeezed her heart, taking her breath away. The most important thing she had learned from him—to forgive the mistakes of the past—was the one lesson he couldn't apply to himself. She slumped against the wall and gave in to the overwhelming need to cry.

"You lied, Clayton," she whispered to the silence. "You promised you'd never leave."

Clayton drove his car around with no destination in mind. He'd berated himself for the last half hour. After years of defending his aunt against any accusations, the joke was on him. She had planned Meg's kidnapping. Maybe if he hadn't been so steadfast in his aunt's defense, Meg might have been found sooner.

He thought about the bitter irony. *Sara was a cousin of Clayton's father.* Mikki had been raised by his family while he had been raised with hers. With one big difference. While he had been learning the proper way to pick French wine for his dinner, she had been learning how to pick pockets for hers.

How could he face Richard? How could he ever face Mikki again?

He pulled his car off the road under a flashing neon sign. Loud music, a smoke-filled bar and a few stiff drinks might dull the ache gnawing at his gut. But after two hours he realized the effort was futile. And worse, the bartender had made him trade his keys for the last drink.

Mikki went to the study to find her father. The more she thought about what to say, the more convinced she was that she had made the right decision. No matter what the reason, Richard would never understand, never forgive. The truth would destroy too many lives in its wake.

Richard was at his desk poring over the reports. He glanced up and smiled. "Meg. Have a seat. Where's Clayton?"

I wish I knew, she thought as she slipped into the chair across from the desk. "He had something to take care of. I'll meet him at home later."

"Oh. He didn't have to get started on things tonight. Now that we've found you, the rest can wait a few days."

"I wanted to talk to you about that."

"What's on your mind?"

She leaned forward and placed her hand on the stack of papers covering his desk. "I don't want the investigation to go any further. It's over."

Lines of confusion creased his forehead as he frowned. "I don't understand."

"You might not want to hear this, but for most of

my life Sara Finnley was the only mother I'd known. I loved her, like I love you.''

''She was involved in your kidnapping,'' he roared, pounding his fist on the solid mahogany desktop.

''And she's dead. Is there a point to destroying her name? It would only hurt her family and, like it or not, I'm one of those people.'' She lowered her gaze.

''Oh, Meg, I don't want to hurt you.''

''Then for my sake, leave it alone.''

He paused for a long moment, then slowly nodded. ''If that's what you want.''

''Please.''

''You have my word.''

Mikki raised a half smile. She sensed her father's reluctance, but she knew instinctively he wouldn't break his word. ''I have to get going. It's a work night. I wouldn't want people at the office to think I was slacking off just because my daddy owns the company. Which reminds me. What do you want me to call you? Dad, Daddy, Father?''

Happily distracted by her question, he puffed his chest out proudly. ''Any one will be fine with me. When will I see you again?''

''I thought I might hang out with you by the pool this weekend.''

''I'll look forward to your visit.''

She grinned and slipped out of the study before her father realized she didn't have a ride home. If he volunteered to take her, he might want to speak with Clayton before she had a chance to. She had no idea if Clayton planned to return to the condo tonight.

In the foyer, she reached for the phone to call a cab.

''Meg?''

At the sound of Joseph's uncertain voice, she replaced the receiver. She turned and braced herself for the worst. "Yeah?"

"I wanted to thank you for what you did back there."

She arched an eyebrow. "Excuse me?"

"I overheard your conversation with Uncle Richard."

A wave of resentment washed over her. "Eavesdropping?"

He cleared his throat. "Yes, well, I was afraid that you might be telling him about my father. I don't care for myself, but my mother..."

She waved her hand. "Forget it."

As she turned to leave, Joseph touched her on the shoulder. The slight, yet unexpected contact surprised her. She stared into the dark eyes of this man who bore a striking physical resemblance to Richard and her.

"I won't forget what you did."

"I didn't do it for you or your mother. I did it for my father."

"Whatever your reasons, Meg, I owe you one."

"Don't be too sure. Sometimes silence is its own worst punishment."

"I know."

She nodded her head sorrowfully. "I believe you do."

Clayton pulled himself up the stairs, an effort that took all the energy he possessed. In the wall mirror he caught the reflection of his disheveled appearance and groaned. He looked a little too much like Joseph on an average Saturday night at the country club.

He shuffled into the living room and sank into the nearest chair. He sat in the darkness, trying to ignore the spinning in his head, as he listened to the distant rumble of waves as they crashed against shore.

A click was followed by a bright light. As his eyes focused, he saw Mikki curled up in the corner of the sofa. "What are you doing here?" he muttered.

"I live here."

Raising his arm over his face, he shielded the light and avoided her gaze. "You should have stayed at your father's."

"Maybe you should have. If you think drowning your sorrows in a bottle of—" she paused and sniffed the air "—scotch will solve anything, you have more in common with my cousins than I do."

"I'm not up to this right now," he mumbled.

"I hope you didn't drive home like that."

"I'm an idiot, but I'm not stupid."

"You could have fooled me."

He let out a bitter laugh. "Apparently I fooled the entire family."

"I'd disagree but I've learned that you can't win an argument with a bottle of scotch." Disgust rang in her voice. He was none too proud of himself, either.

"Go home."

"I am home. And when you sleep it off, we are going to talk."

He laid a hand across his churning stomach.

She laughed at his discomfort. "I hope you spend the night hugging the toilet. It's nothing less than you deserve."

"I deserve that and a lot more."

She sprung to her feet and covered the distance between them. "Yeah. You deserve a kick in the rear end, you hypocrite."

"Care to explain that?"

"Sure. When you're sober enough to understand. I'm going to bed. I have to work tomorrow."

She stroked her fingers across his forehead and through the hair at his temple. The tender gesture sent a live current straight to his groin. The sad part was, if he acted on his desires she probably wouldn't stop him. Why did she have to be so damned forgiving? She brushed a kiss against his cheek and walked away. A slap across the face would have hurt less.

A loud clatter woke Clayton from a restless sleep. As a blinding light flooded the room, pain ricocheted through his brain. He grunted and buried his face in the pillows.

"Good morning." Mikki's perky voice sent another jolt of pain through him.

In his present, hungover condition, he couldn't face her. Who was he kidding? His condition had nothing to do with it. How could he get through to her? He didn't want forgiveness. He wanted the blame.

She sat on the edge of the bed and yanked the covers off him. "Here."

He raised his head and peered out through heavy eyelids. She held a cup toward him. "What's that? A hair of the dog that bit me?"

"That dog didn't bite you. He mauled you. It's water for the aspirin."

As he struggled to sit up, he modestly covered himself with a pillow.

She laughed. "Are you hiding something I haven't seen before?"

"Mikki," he grumbled.

"Take the aspirin and go back to sleep for a while." Her voice sounded weary, as if she hadn't slept any better than he had. The desire to pull her into his arms and rock her to sleep nearly overcame him, until he reminded himself that he didn't have that right.

He swallowed the tablets with a large gulp of water. They might help the dull ache in his head, but they wouldn't cure the sharp pain in his heart. The guilt he had lived with most of his life paled in comparison to what he felt now. She and Richard had a lifetime to catch up on. He wasn't worthy of a part in it.

"I have to go or I'll miss my bus."

"You're going to work today?"

A smile brightened her entire face. "Would you like me to call in sick and we'll spend the morning in bed?"

He would like nothing more than to lose himself with her. And then what? Avoid her father the rest of his life? Put her in a position where she had to choose between them? "I don't think that's a good idea."

"I'm seeing the side effects of your last good idea. At least mine doesn't cause a hangover." She pulled the blanket across his body, gently tucking the edges around him. "I'll see you later."

Fifteen

Clayton massaged his throbbing temples. Three times he had started to write his resignation. No easy feat since his head was pounding and he couldn't type. Two messages from Alicia went unanswered.

Meetings had kept him occupied most of the afternoon. With the office nearly empty, he gave his full attention to the letter and tried to convince himself that resigning was the right thing to do. The company ran smoothly. Although Richard had stayed in the background the past few years, he had kept himself apprised of policy changes.

Clayton thought about the ironic twist of fate. He had always imagined he'd be fighting to hold on to his position. The company was a part of him. In a way, his retribution to Richard for Meg's kidnapping. Perhaps it was fitting that he leave now.

He drummed his fingers against the desktop. No

words seemed adequate. Before he finished the first paragraph, he was interrupted by a loud knock. Without waiting for a response, Joseph strode into the office.

"Is the polo club closed today?" Clayton asked.

"I guess I deserve that." Joseph prowled around the room like a nervous panther, then balanced himself on the edge of a chair. "I want to talk to you about a job."

Clayton looked up from the keyboard. "Is this a joke? You have a job."

"I get a paycheck. It's not the same as having a job."

"And why are you talking to me?"

"Oh, come on, Clay. It's your company. It has been for years."

"It's Richard's company. And one day it will be Mikki's."

"She doesn't want it. You know that as well as I do. She wants to save the whales. And Richard wants to spend his time getting to know Meg again."

Apparently Joseph took more interest in his family than Clayton had credited him. Without his father's oppressive shadow hanging over him, Joseph was finally coming into his own.

"You want to work? Try sales. They need help."

"Sales," Joseph repeated. "That would suit me."

"Good. Was that all?"

"No. I wanted to talk to you about a family matter."

Clayton shook his head. When had his status been elevated to a member of the family? "What?"

"I need to know what *you* plan to do." Joseph cracked his knuckles together. "Even though Meg asked Richard not to pursue an investigation—"

"She did?"

"I figured she told you. Anyway, I know I don't have the right to ask any favors of you. But since Meg doesn't want answers, I'd like to spare my mother from further humiliation." Obviously, Joseph was afraid his father had been involved in the abduction. Clayton thought to correct him but David Hawthorne owned as much responsibility as Alicia.

"I won't be digging around in the past anymore."

So, Mikki had gone to her father to protect his aunt. Clayton wondered if Alicia would go to Richard on her own or respect Mikki's wishes.

"You know, Meg is probably the most decent member of this family, despite the way she grew up," Joseph noted.

"Too bad she wasn't afforded the same privileges we were."

"If she had been, she would have turned out like the rest of us." He shrugged. "I better get going. You were obviously in the middle of something."

Once he had the office to himself, Clayton reread the first paragraph. Was his leaving in everyone's best interest or a coward's retreat? Richard had no wish to run the company again. He wanted time with his daughter. Time he would have if Clayton convinced Mikki to return home. She wouldn't get any more grief from her cousins.

There was still the matter of getting Mikki to agree. He tried to recall one occasion when he had won an argument with her. Strong-willed, stubborn and passionate about her beliefs, she rarely gave up and never gave in.

Mikki paused outside the office door and peeked inside. Clayton was staring at the computer screen, but he appeared to be lost in thought. She cleared her throat to get his attention.

His head shot up. "Mikki. Why are you still here?"

She strode into the room with more confidence than she felt. "I need to talk to you."

"Here?"

"I would have waited until later, but I wasn't sure if you were coming home or just stopping off at the nearest bar."

"Oh." He looked repentant and still a bit hungover. "Have a seat. I need to talk to you, too."

She perched herself on the edge of his desk, leaning forward to meet his unwavering gaze. "If any of this starts with, 'I think you should move back with your father,' save your breath."

"Be reasonable."

"I'm not the one who suffers from a lack of reason."

He exhaled deeply. "You don't understand."

"I do." She laid her hand on his shoulder and drew hope from the fact that he didn't recoil. "You feel guilty about what you think I lost. But I never missed what I never had."

"I can't forget what my aunt did to you."

"So, you're disappointed and angry with Alicia, and I'm going to be punished for it?"

"I don't mean to hurt you."

She blinked back a tear that threatened to fall. "Well, you are."

His eyes narrowed sorrowfully. "You'll see this is for the best."

"Who appointed you the keeper of my best interests?"

"I'm sorry." He rose and stepped around the desk. "I need some space right now."

"How much space? Different bedrooms or different zip codes?"

He remained silent.

She slipped into the chair he vacated and folded her arms on the desk. Running headfirst into a granite wall would be more productive and less painful than trying to reason with Clayton. She glanced up at his computer screen and read the opening paragraph.

"Oh, this is nice," she snapped. "Not only do you plan to walk out on me, you plan to walk out on Richard, too."

"I'm not walking out." He hit the Delete button and cleared the screen.

"I hope not. Because I promise you one thing. I don't blame you for the last twenty years, but if you walk out of my life now, I'll blame you for the next twenty years."

Without waiting for his reaction, she left the office. He needed time to think. After all, it had only been twenty-four hours since his long-held beliefs had been shattered. He had given her more time than that to get used to her new circumstances.

On her way out of the building she met Joseph. To her surprise, he offered her a ride, and to his visible surprise, she accepted. At the condo she changed her clothes and stuffed a few articles in her backpack. If Clayton needed space, she'd give him space.

Clayton picked up the receiver for the hundredth time and once again discarded the idea. What if she hadn't gone to her father's house? What would he tell

Richard? *Sorry, sir, I seem to have lost your daughter again.* Damn! Why hadn't she left him a message?

He had spent a restless night wondering and worrying about Mikki. The exhaustion of the past few days was catching up with him. He couldn't sleep, he couldn't eat. Hell, he couldn't think straight anymore.

By the time he finally convinced himself that she had gone home, Richard called, asking for her. So much for that brilliant theory. Where had she gone? He had worked himself into an irrational state. When she walked in the front door, he lost what little control he'd still possessed.

"Where the hell have you been?"

She dropped her backpack at his feet. "Camping."

"Alone?"

"No. I took the Boston Red Sox with me."

"Very funny." He had worried himself sick and she was cracking jokes.

"Of course I went alone. You said you needed some space. I gave you three thousand square feet of space. Did you enjoy yourself in my absence?"

"You couldn't leave a note?"

"I told Alicia where I went."

His muscles tensed. Mikki knew he wouldn't call his aunt. He was surprised she had. "Your father called a few minutes ago. He's expecting you this afternoon."

"I know. I just stopped by to get my bathing suit."

"So, you'll be back later?"

The corner of her mouth lifted in a knowing grin. "You want me to come back, don't you?"

Yes. No. He didn't know. Why couldn't she react in an outraged and indignant manner like a normal person? Her unconditional love made him feel worse. She should hate him at least as much as he hated himself right now. "Well, I don't want you to live in a tent."

She wound her arms around his neck and pressed against him. The silky strands of her lemon-scented hair tickled his neck as she snuggled closer. "Come with me today."

Oh, Lord, she was hard to resist. His body had already surrendered. His mind was slipping fast. Before he lost himself completely, he gently pushed her back. "I'd rather not."

"Fine. Stay home alone and be miserable."

"I don't see how you can just forget what Alicia did to you."

"Because I'm alive." Her voice was pitched to reflect the depth of her belief. "I don't know if David Hawthorne would have been caught before he succeeded, and neither do you."

"There had to be another way besides condemning you to a life of hell."

She blew a puff of air to lift the wisps of bangs from her forehead. "My life was not the hell you imagine. My mom was good to me. Even Max had his moments."

"That doesn't change the fact that you lost your childhood with your father. You should spend time with him now, enjoying the things you missed."

"And I will. That doesn't mean I can't spend time with you, too. I am capable of sustaining two concurrent relationships. As much as I like the idea, I can't keep you pinned to the sheets every second of the day."

"So you want me for the sex?"

"You're damn right, but that's not the only reason.

Don't you get it yet? I love you. Without you, life wouldn't be fun anymore.''

''It's not supposed to be.''

''Yes, it is. Otherwise, why bother?''

He rolled his eyes skyward for help from above. ''You're not making this easy.''

''You want me to make it easy for you to leave me? I'll make it simple. Tell me you don't love me, and I'll be out the door before you can blink.''

''This isn't about love.''

''Buzz. Wrong answer. You're stuck with me.''

''Mikki!''

''Oh, Clayton.'' She whirled around and let out an exasperated sigh. ''I am exhausted from arguing with you. I'm going to my father's. If you need to make some radical change in your life to get over this, then get a tattoo or go buy a Harley-Davidson. Whatever it takes. When you're ready to accept that we belong together, come get me.''

After she left, he walked around his three thousand square feet of space feeling alone and empty. Signs of Mikki were everywhere. Seashells on the nightstand, starfish on the coffee table. Even a bouquet of dandelion flowers, beautiful in its simplicity. A lot like the woman herself, he thought. In the short time she had been living with him, she had left a lasting mark, in his home, in his life and mostly in his heart.

Mikki watched the tennis ball whiz by her. She wiped a hand across her forehead and let out a laugh. Three straight sets and she hadn't been able to return one serve. She should have known better than to accept a challenge when she had no idea how to play the game, but she couldn't refuse the friendly gesture from

Joseph. Even William had grunted a hello in her direction today. A definite improvement over their last meetings. They might not be the Cleaver family, but they were *her* family.

"Forty-love," Joseph called out as another ball flew by.

"I hate this game," she grumbled to the clay court.

Richard, sitting in a lawn chair as the line judge, smiled indulgently. "You just need a few lessons."

"No, thank you." She tipped her sun visor to Joseph and skipped off the court. "What kind of game is this, anyway? The scoring is all messed up. And who was the rocket scientist who decided that love is nothing. Love is everything. That should be the highest score."

He laughed. "Missing Clayton?"

She shrugged indifferently, but she missed him more with each passing hour.

"Why don't you go to the club with Joseph and watch the polo match," Richard suggested.

"No way," her cousin cut in. "She'd be lecturing us on why the horses should be set free."

"Polo?" she said and raised an eyebrow. "It's field hockey on horseback because you're too lazy to run around yourself."

"Told you," Joseph muttered and started to walk away. "And speaking of lazy, the next time I need a nap, I'll call you for another match."

She bent down, snatched a tennis ball and lobbed it successfully into his back. "Fifteen-Love."

"You're still a little brat, Meg," he taunted, and sprinted away before she could reach for another ball.

"I'm happy to see the two of you getting along," Richard said. He rose and walked with Mikki toward the house.

"Sure. It's easy to be congenial when he wins. He wiped the court with me."

"Well, you are pathetic." He draped an arm across her shoulder. "At tennis, I mean."

"Gee, thanks, Dad."

"I told you I could arrange for lessons."

"Oh, great. Some pampered country club pro in those silly white shorts is going to show me how to improve my backhand technique."

"I don't know how to tell you, Meg. You have no backhand technique."

"No, but she has a wicked left hook."

"Clayton!" Mikki spun around. Her heartbeat accelerated at the sight of him. Dressed in jeans and a black T-shirt, he looked nothing like the stuffy yuppie she had left at the condo a few hours ago.

"You're early, Clay," Richard said.

"I am?"

"Mikki said you wouldn't be here until six."

"Oh, she did?" Clayton sounded mildly amused. "You were that sure of me?"

She shook her head. "Wishful thinking on my part."

Richard cocked his eyebrow in confusion. "Am I missing something?" Neither she nor Clayton answered as they stared at each other. "Am I interrupting something?"

"May I borrow your daughter?" Clayton didn't wait for a reply. He caught Mikki's wrist and pulled her to him. She smiled her goodbye as he tugged her along.

"Where are we going?"

He led her across the lawn and around the perimeter of the house in silence. She studied his face, trying to gauge his mood. Although he had seemed relaxed just a few seconds ago, he now looked anxious. What was going through his mind?

Mikki planted her feet firmly and refused to move. "I'm not taking another step until you tell me what's going on."

"All right." He clasped his hands around her waist, urging her closer with his sheer strength. Rough denim brushed against her legs.

She sighed longingly. "Okay. This is nice."

Coils of heat rippled through her. Oh, he felt good! The heady scent of musk left her dizzy. He cuddled her tighter in his embrace. The front yard was an odd place for an interlude, she thought, but she wasn't about to complain.

She locked her arms around his neck and kissed him fiercely. All her pent-up feelings of frustration and fear melted away as he returned the hungry kiss.

Clayton reluctantly lifted his mouth from hers. She let out a soft moan of protest, and her eyes rounded wide in surprise. She stared for several seconds.

"You've pierced your ear," she suddenly exclaimed in delight. She ran her finger over the diamond stud.

"Back in college. My big stab at liberation lasted the first semester. I was too afraid to go home with an earring."

"I like it."

His smile broadened. "I thought you might. I spent half an hour trying to push that earring through."

"So, are you okay now?" He heard the hope in her voice.

"Not yet." He stroked his finger along her cheek, prompting a sigh from her. "You told me to do whatever it takes to get over it."

"And?"

"First of all, you can finish out the summer, but once college begins, you're fired."

"What?"

"I won't feel right unless you get the same advantages Richard gave the rest of us. College is a full-time job. You'll have enough trouble balancing classes, your father and me. You don't have to hold down a job, too."

"Is this negotiable?"

"No. That's the deal. Take it or leave it."

"What am I supposed to do for money?"

"I think we'll scrape by without your income until you finish college."

She didn't looked pleased by the prospect. That was Mikki. She never wanted what most people would want.

"You said you would do whatever it takes," he reminded her.

She shook her head. "That's not fair."

"Don't talk to me about fair," he grumbled. "Nothing about your life has been fair."

She tried unsuccessfully to suppress a mischievous grin. "My life hasn't been so bad since you came crashing into it."

"So, what do you say?"

"I wouldn't feel right living off your money, Clayton."

"A lot of husbands put their wives through school. It will all balance in the end when you start working again."

"We're not married."

"We will be," he stated matter-of-factly.

Her foot landed pointedly on top of his. She

wouldn't let that one slip by. "Oh, yeah. And did you plan to ask me?"

He exhaled the breath he'd been holding. "I thought I just had."

"It sounded more like a business proposal. Where was the romance? The flowers and candy? The trinkets of everlasting devotion?"

"You need trinkets. I'll give you trinkets. Come on."

He placed his arm firmly across her back and propelled her forward. Once they rounded the corner and stepped onto the driveway, he let her go. "Is that a big enough trinket?"

She stared at the four-wheel-drive Jeep with the large red ribbon covering the front windshield. "What's this?"

"I thought you would like it better than a car. Your camping gear will fit in the back."

"You bought it for me?" she whispered as if she were unable to believe the possibility. "Why?"

"You'll need to get to your classes every day."

She circled the vehicle.

"You don't like it?" he asked.

"What's not to like? But…"

"No buts. It's your wedding present."

She arched her eyebrow seductively. "Can I take it for a test drive before I make a decision?"

"No. I'm saving it for after the wedding."

"Oh, Clayton. You're so old-fashioned. I guess that's why I love you."

"Does that mean you'll marry me?"

She flung herself into his arms. "Yes. But I have a few conditions of my own."

"Like?"

"I want Alicia to stand up for me at my wedding. Do you have a problem with that?"

"Do I have a choice?"

"You have to forgive her."

"Why?"

"Because you won't forgive yourself until you do. And I would hate to think you were marrying me out of guilt. That's not how I want to have you."

"I'm marrying you because I love you," he insisted. Although he had never subscribed to the Machiavellian theory that the end justified the means, Mikki was alive today. His aunt had acted with noble, albeit misguided, intentions. If Mikki could forgive Alicia, he could, too. "All right. I'll talk to her."

"You'll be happier."

"You've agreed to be my wife. I couldn't be happier."

"You think not?" She snuggled closer, torturing him with her deliberate twisting movements. "Take me for a ride in my new truck and I'll show you heaven."

He scanned the area to make sure no one was watching. "After we get married, I'm going to teach you some self-control."

Her hand caressed the bulging fabric of his jeans. "No, you won't. Because around you, I don't want to have self-control. I want to be able to touch you wherever and whenever I want to. That's the deal. Take it or leave it."

The woman drove a hard bargain, in more ways than one. He hesitated for a moment, then reached for the door of the Jeep. "I can live with that."

Epilogue

"**G**ood luck, Clayton." Joseph paused at the door and smiled wryly.

"Don't you mean congratulations?"

"Knowing Meg, I mean good luck." Joseph's laughter echoed down the corridor.

Clayton chuckled and switched off his computer. Hopefully he had covered everything. If not, any problem would have to wait a couple of weeks. He had a honeymoon to attend, and Mikki had threatened to sledgehammer his cellular phone if he tried to sneak it into the luggage. Not that he would have the time or the interest for company affairs while he had her alone in the mountains.

He locked his briefcase then left the office without it. The customer service department had taken Mikki out for a bachelorette party. He was afraid to ask where, and she didn't volunteer the information. Without her, he wasn't anxious to go home, but hanging around an empty office held less appeal.

As he walked down the hall, he heard a noise coming from the conference room. It was too early for the cleaning staff and too late on a Friday for even the most diligent worker. He pushed the door open.

"'Bout time," Mikki said. She sat cross-legged on the conference table, wearing a satin teddy and high heels. Her skirt and blouse were tossed in a careless heap on a chair. "I thought you were going to spend the night in your office."

"What are you doing?"

"Today was my last day of work before my forced resignation."

He choked back a laugh. She made it sound as if he had sentenced her to death rather than making her life easier when she began her classes in a couple of weeks. "I thought you were out celebrating your last day of freedom. What happened to the party?"

She held up a folded dollar bill. "I'd much rather stuff this down your briefs than the Incredible Stud's G-string. That way, I can get it back later."

"They took you to see a male stripper? Remind me to fire the customer service department when we get back."

Her tongue ran provocatively along her bottom lip. "Don't worry. He had nothing over you."

"You're getting married tomorrow. Don't you have things to do?"

"Like Alicia and my dad would trust me with the details of my wedding? As long as I show up at the church wearing white, I don't have to do anything." Mikki exaggerated, but not by much.

Clayton only went along with the elaborate wedding

plans because Richard had missed out on so many other events in his daughter's life. He stepped closer to the oak table and gestured to her with his finger. "Come here."

She slid over to the end of the table and wrapped her legs around his hips. Her fingers worked the knot of his tie with ease. She made quick work of his jacket, too.

"What do you think you're doing?"

"This is my last chance," she said, while continuing to undress him. The shirt fell from his shoulders.

"Last chance for what?"

"To see if you really are better in the boardroom than the bedroom."

"You can't be serious?" His question was rhetorical, since she showed no sign of backing down.

"Lighten up. It will be fun."

"We could be home in twenty minutes."

"We could be naked in twenty seconds." Her gaze traveled lower, and his pulse rate soared. She made a good point and a damned inviting one.

How did she talk him into these things? He would never be able to use the room again without thinking about making love to her. She probably knew it, too.

"This is insane." He unsnapped the teddy and probed the damp folds of skin between her legs. Her body shuddered in response.

"Totally crazy," she muttered as she fumbled for his belt buckle.

His pants dropped to the floor. "I should have my head examined by a doctor."

She drew her pink fingernail down the center of his chest, then traced the same line with her tongue. How he loved the way she touched him!

"Would you settle for having your body examined by me?"

"Examine away, Doctor." He raised his arms above his head to give her full access. "And make sure you're thorough."

"It could take time to explore you thoroughly."

"We've got a lifetime."

*   *   *   *   *

If you enjoyed what you just read,
then we've got an offer you can't resist!

Take 2 bestselling love stories FREE!

Plus get a FREE surprise gift!

Clip this page and mail it to Silhouette Reader Service™

IN U.S.A.	IN CANADA
3010 Walden Ave.	P.O. Box 609
P.O. Box 1867	Fort Erie, Ontario
Buffalo, N.Y. 14240-1867	L2A 5X3

YES! Please send me 2 free Silhouette Desire® novels and my free surprise gift. Then send me 6 brand-new novels every month, which I will receive months before they're available in stores. In the U.S.A., bill me at the bargain price of $3.12 plus 25¢ delivery per book and applicable sales tax, if any*. In Canada, bill me at the bargain price of $3.49 plus 25¢ delivery per book and applicable taxes**. That's the complete price and a savings of over 10% off the cover prices—what a great deal! I understand that accepting the 2 free books and gift places me under no obligation ever to buy any books. I can always return a shipment and cancel at any time. Even if I never buy another book from Silhouette, the 2 free books and gift are mine to keep forever. So why not take us up on our invitation. You'll be glad you did!

225 SEN CNFA
326 SEN CNFC

Name _____ (PLEASE PRINT)

Address _____ Apt.# _____

City _____ State/Prov. _____ Zip/Postal Code _____

* Terms and prices subject to change without notice. Sales tax applicable in N.Y.
** Canadian residents will be charged applicable provincial taxes and GST.
   All orders subject to approval. Offer limited to one per household.
   ® are registered trademarks of Harlequin Enterprises Limited.

DES99   ©1998 Harlequin Enterprises Limited

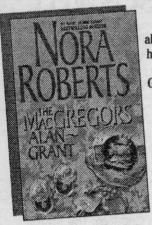
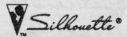

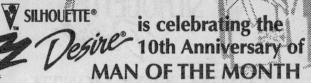

SILHOUETTE® Desire®

COMING NEXT MONTH